FAUX REEL

FAUX REEL

An Imogene Museum Mystery
Book 5

JERUSHA JONES

THOMAS & MERCER

Published by Thomas & Mercer, Seattle
www.apub.com

Amazon, the Amazon logo, and Thomas & Mercer are trademarks of Amazon.com, Inc., or its affiliates.

ISBN-13: 9781477829240
ISBN-10: 1477829245

Cover design by Elizabeth Berry MacKenney

Printed in the United States of America

CHAPTER 1

I sashayed Jesamie Stettler through the bowels of the Imogene Museum. She's Sheriff Marge's new granddaughter, and she's adorable in a squat, elfin way—when she's not screaming. Something about the general hubbub and crowd of strangers at our first annual fundraiser had set her off, however, and she was venting the full force of her tiny lungs in protest.

Her parents and grandmother had exhausted their resources, so I claimed a turn and took Jesamie to the far end of the old mansion, hoping her distress wouldn't disturb the other guests. Her tears and slobber soaked the front of my coral-colored silk gown, but it was still less mess than I'm accustomed to as the museum's curator—I'm usually up to my elbows in centuries-old grime. Not in an evening gown, though.

The taxidermy exhibit housed in the library did the trick. A dusty black bear standing on its hind feet with bared teeth is kind of like a teddy bear, right? Jesamie considered the idea. She stared, wide-eyed, and gulped back sobs.

Next up, a snarling cougar poised in a crouch on a realistic-looking pile of plastic boulders. The taxidermist had artfully extended the big cat's claws in the pose, even though cougars normally keep the business end of their toes retracted. Jesamie rubbed her nose hard on my bare shoulder, smearing goop all over both of us.

"Hey, kiddo." I shifted Jesamie higher on my hip and patted her back. "Why don't you fall asleep? Then you won't be so miserable." As if logic could convince an infant.

I tucked her downy head under my chin and sang the closest thing I could think of to a lullaby—Louis Armstrong's version of "Dream a Little Dream of Me," complete with deep, raspy voice. I totally faked it—not well, apparently—and garnered another wide-eyed stare. Babies must think adults are complete idiots.

We wandered through the petroglyph and pictograph replica displays, Wishram and Klickitat woven baskets, Victorian ball gowns, and Indonesian pottery. No one would ever pay to listen to me sing, but after the initial shock, Jesamie didn't seem to mind. Finally, in the chamber pot exhibit, her little body went limp, disrupted occasionally by a hiccup.

I was singing only because we were alone, and because Jesamie wouldn't remember a thing about it by the time she's old enough to talk. The majority of the guests were occupied with the current demonstration out on the museum's expansive lawn. I'd lost track, but it was either mountain-man survival skills or metal detecting or calf roping. Like the Imogene's exhibits, the evening's educational programs were diverse, eclectic, and hands-on, and the attendees seemed to be having a great time.

I had to admit the idea of starting a campfire with flint and kindling, or firing a shotgun loaded with wadding while in your black-tie best, held a certain appeal, especially for the city-bred male guests. I hoped they would show their appreciation with their checkbooks later on.

Given Jesamie's relaxed state, I thought I might be able to sneak a quick check on the collection of sabretaches en route from Hungary. Because we all know the more often you track a highly anticipated shipment, the faster it moves. Crooning softly, I creaked up the stairs to the third floor, then stopped in front of my office door, pondering the few inches it hung open. I was certain I'd closed it—and locked it.

I poked the door with a forefinger, and it swung open on squealing hinges. My desk looked the way it always does—messy. My laptop sat blinking in power-saving mode. None of the piles on the floor seemed to have been disturbed. I stepped into the room and scanned the bookshelves lining the walls—nothing was obviously missing. Maybe I'd been careless that afternoon, distracted by the upcoming event and worried about being able to squeeze into my dress.

Jesamie whimpered, and I knew I couldn't risk sitting. Frowning, I flicked off the light, latched the door, and locked it. I had to keep moving, keep the comforting swaying going for Jesamie.

I two-stepped a few feet down the hall, then came up short in front of an ornate, gold-leafed—and empty—picture frame. My mouth fell open. Ragged canvas threads jutted from the inner sides of the frame. The painting, a big one—54 by 72 inches—had been cut out with a dull blade.

I stood, breath frozen in my chest, too long for Jesamie's unpracticed patience. She whined and wriggled, turning her head to stare along with me at the gaping hole. Then she dissolved into loud wails. I was too shocked for tears.

The missing painting was hideous. And I'm not exaggerating. It had been beautiful only in the eyes of its long-dead creator. Why anyone else would think it was worth hanging, let alone worth stealing, was beyond me.

I'd moved the painting in my first week on the job—I hated it that much. Originally, it had hung in a place of prominence in the ballroom, the main hall visitors enter first. I'd snuck it away to this remote location where few tourists ever ventured.

We were stuck with the painting because the artist, of the founding Hagg family lineage, had bequeathed it, along with a large sum of money, to the museum with the stipulation that it always be on public display. He'd failed to say exactly where the painting was to be exhibited, and I took advantage of that loophole.

Rupert Hagg, the museum's director, had applauded my action. "You got rid of that awful thing, I see," he'd said. "Good riddance."

I'd felt bad explaining that the painting wasn't—and couldn't be—completely disposed of but that it was out of the main traffic flow.

"Good enough," Rupert had huffed, because his office is on the second floor and he only rarely climbs to the third. "It gives me the willies."

Dead fish willies. You know those still lifes by the great masters—the ones with bloody, lifeless pheasants, blue-and-white pitchers and piles of fruit, maybe a crumbled loaf of bread and a cornucopia—that are supposed to portray abundance and contentment and the good life? Yeah, well, substitute a gasping, bulgy-eyed salmon for the pheasant, glistening chicken-gut bait for the fruit, a fishing creel for the cornucopia with a rod and reel in the background, and you'd have a pretty good idea of our gifted monstrosity.

And that's just the subject matter. The technique lent another level to the hodgepodge—literally. The artist had used a combination of thick acrylic paint and decoupage to create a disgusting depth of field so the salmon seemed about to slither off the canvas and onto your lap. The reel was exceptionally realistic, with bits of tangled fishing line glued in place. Everyone who saw the painting instinctively took a step backward.

And now it was gone.

So was the money that had been donated along with it decades ago, so maybe it didn't matter.

Except that someone had stolen it. And if they could steal this painting, what else could they—or did they—abscond with?

I'd already started to worry about the burgeoning value of our collections. They're odd, to be sure, but dedicated niche collectors have been known to drop crazy sums on items to round out their private specimen assortment. Many of our individual pieces were probably worth tens of thousands, with some complete collections well into the middle six figures.

Just as abruptly as she'd started, Jesamie quit crying. She stuck a corner of her fist in her mouth, sucking noisily.

I hurried down the hall and pushed through the swinging door to the servants' stairwell. If I want to get anywhere in the museum fast, I take the servants' stairwell—the direct and discreet arterial access to the old mansion's main living areas, which also happens to be closed to the public.

Clomping noisily in my strappy high heels, I lumbered down the wood stairs, Jesamie's head bobbing in time with my lurching gait. At the first landing, I kicked something hard and metallic, sending it skittering.

"Ow!" I pulled up the knee of the leg attached to my smarting toes and balanced, wobbling, like a heron. "Blast and poot," I said through gritted teeth.

Jesamie took her fingers out of her mouth long enough to give me a toothless grin.

"Oh, you think that's funny, huh? I'm not going to be the one who corrupts your vocabulary." I dodged my head around, trying to see what I'd hit.

A box knife, blade extended, lay at the base of a banister post.

I quickly checked my toes—already bright red and swollen, but no blood. Apparently I hadn't kicked the knife on the blade end.

Using the hem of my dress like a handkerchief, I scooped up the box knife. Maybe the thief's fingerprints were on it. And if it *was* the thief's, then he knew a lot about the mansion's layout and floor plan. His level of preparation and timing made the knot in my stomach even bigger.

ooo

I spotted Sheriff Marge in a corner of the ballroom, near the buffet tables. The demonstration outside must have ended, because the room was packed with people in tuxedos and brightly colored gowns, but Sheriff Marge's khaki uniform and big Stratton hat were easy to pick out. I've never seen her in anything else. I imagine she sleeps in them, too. I hope she at least removes the pointy bits, like the badge and gun belt, before relaxing.

I sidled through the crowd with my arms wrapped protectively around Jesamie. She seemed to have gotten over her initial discomfiture about all the strangers, though, and she swiveled her little head around, taking it all in. I heard several murmured "cutie pie" and "sweetheart" comments, which I'm pretty sure were for her benefit and not mine.

I slid into the conversation circle beside Sheriff Marge. Her face lit up when she saw Jesamie, and I transferred the baby to her grand-mother's arms.

I was desperate to tell Sheriff Marge about the theft, but there was no way I would do so publicly, not at our first fundraising event. I tried giving her a meaningful look and tipping my head toward the kitchen. But Sheriff Marge was absorbed with wiping Jesamie's nose, so I was left giving the impression I have a nervous tic. I plastered on a smile for the others in the group.

Sheriff Marge stuffed the tissue in her pocket. "Meredith Morehouse, curator of the Imogene." Sheriff Marge pointed at me. "This is Melvin Sharpe." She nodded to a tall, swarthy man with old-school 1950s glasses who looked like he didn't know what to do with his feet. He kept bending his knees, dipping and rising, with lips pursed.

Melvin extended a knuckly hand, which I shook.

"He's a documentary filmmaker and just arrived. He's scouting Platts Landing as a potential location for his next project."

"Really?" My brows shot up. "What settings do you need?" Documentaries are usually low-budget affairs, so I didn't hold out hope for a big payout, but the exposure might be good for the museum.

"Oh—" Melvin cleared his throat. "Fields and crops maybe a vineyard or two and fruit eating—" He didn't speak with punctuation. All his words ran together and then just faded. I held my breath and leaned forward, waiting for him to finish, but he did the dip-and-bob thing again and clasped his hands behind his back.

I glanced at Sheriff Marge. Her mouth was clamped shut as she focused on adjusting Jesamie's ruffled dress.

I scowled and turned back to Melvin. "What's your subject?"

"Oh—how people make food you know the plants it grows on and not shrink-wrapped packages like the real thing—"

Sheriff Marge doesn't laugh often, but when she does, it's worth being present for. She emitted a stifled snort, then started jiggling in a solid vibration, her movement somewhat suppressed by the Kevlar vest under her uniform shirt. Jesamie's little arms flapped with the bouncing, as though she were about to take flight.

"Doesn't her diaper need changing or something?" I hissed at Sheriff Marge.

She snuck a thumb behind her ever-present reading glasses and wiped away a tear. "Right." She nodded to the group. "Folks." She spun on her heel and forged a wide path toward the restrooms.

"Awfully nice to meet you." I lunged toward Melvin, grabbed his hand, and shook it again. "Let me know if the museum can be of assistance, and please eat more chili." I waved toward the buffet tables and ducked to follow Sheriff Marge before the wake she'd left closed in.

CHAPTER 2

My trajectory was snarled by politely chatting guests—it seemed the entire county had turned out, plus a huge number of people I didn't recognize. Frankie Cortland, the Imogene's gift shop manager and conscripted event planner, had outdone herself. The evening was already a social success. I was waiting to see if it was a financial success, but the theft turned any celebration I might have been thinking of into a calamity.

I finally located Sheriff Marge in the staff kitchen.

"Her diaper's fine." Sheriff Marge frowned. "I thought you'd want to talk to that filmmaker."

"You dumped him on me. He's surprised food grows on plants? Good grief. But this is worse." I grabbed her arm and checked the doorway to make sure no one was lurking. "A painting's been stolen."

Sheriff Marge's brows shot up. She shifted Jesamie to the opposite hip and whipped a little notebook out of her chest pocket. "Tonight? Or did you just notice tonight?"

I bit my lip. "I can't be sure. I walk past it all the time, but there's no appreciating it, so I don't stop and gaze. I'm sure it was there last

Monday, but since then I couldn't confirm." I mentally chewed myself out. This is my museum—why hadn't I been paying attention?

I dropped the box knife on the lunch table. My palm was sweaty from gripping it during my recent social interactions. Good thing I'd picked it up in my left hand and kept it wrapped in silk, and that my skirt was full enough for me not to look like a major fashion faux pas while doing it.

"I found this in the servants' stairwell. Since the painting was cut out, I thought it might be helpful. I don't leave open box knives lying around—it's not mine."

"You got Ziploc bags?" Sheriff Marge started rummaging through drawers. "I'll tag it."

"I thought I saw you dodge in here." Strong arms encircled my waist from behind and pulled me close. "Sorry I'm late," he murmured against my cheek.

I inhaled. Pete smells so good—licorice and faintly spicy aftershave tonight, a combination that reminded me of Christmas fruitcake. I should mention that I'm probably one of the few people on the planet who actually look forward to holiday fruitcake deliveries. He must have just shaved. If we'd been alone, I'd have gone in for a nuzzle, but my mind snapped back to the matter at hand.

"Third drawer down," I told Sheriff Marge.

Pete turned me by my shoulders. "What's wrong?"

Wow, he looked good, too. I have no idea where he got the tuxedo, but wow, wow, wow. I grinned into his crinkle-cornered, sapphire-blue eyes, then quickly sobered.

"A painting's been stolen," I whispered.

"What is this—a private party in the kitchen?" Rupert Hagg's deep, gravelly voice boomed from the doorway.

"Shhhh." I pulled him into the room and closed the door. It doesn't have a lock, so I leaned against it.

Putting it mildly, Rupert is portly. I think his tuxedo fit him properly about forty pounds ago. His waistcoat strained across his midsection, with gaps between the buttons. At least his jacket hem hung below his bum—I didn't want to see what was happening to the seat of his pants. His everyday outfit is comfortable tweeds. Tonight he looked like an overstuffed sushi roll.

Rupert glanced at each of us in turn, his flushed face falling by degrees. His patent-leather shoes squeaked as he crossed the black-and-white-checked linoleum and dropped into a metal folding chair. "Tell me."

Sheriff Marge nodded at me. I would get to do the honors.

I took a deep breath. "A painting's been stolen." I wondered how many more times I'd have to say those words.

Rupert gripped his knees, propping himself up. "Which one? Only one?"

"Only one that I know of. I'll have to do a complete inventory"—I gestured over my shoulder toward the kitchen door and beyond, toward the swarm of festive guests—"tomorrow. And the next day. And the next . . ."

Rupert watched me steadily, waiting for the bad news.

"The Cosmo Hagg still life, from the third floor."

Rupert's eyes bulged. "That? Whatever for?" he spluttered. "The frame it's in is worth more than the painting."

"Which they left," I said. "They cut the canvas out."

Rupert went beet red, hacking out a sound between grunting and choking. I stretched toward him and placed a hand on his shoulder, but he waved me away. Then I realized he was laughing—hard—and tears streamed down his face.

"Who knew it would come to this?" he wheezed. "I've hated that thing for years."

"Insurance value?" Sheriff Marge asked.

"No need," Rupert gasped. "Perhaps we should offer a reward to the person brave enough to steal it."

Jesamie whimpered, clearly bored with the goings-on, then tested a few screeches in the echoey room.

I could tell from Sheriff Marge's narrowed eyes that she was confounded by Rupert's reaction. "I'll get you a picture of the missing painting and a complete description," I hollered over Jesamie. Sheriff Marge must have never seen the painting in person; otherwise, she'd remember it.

The kitchen door swung open and Hallie Stettler, Sheriff Marge's daughter-in-law, stuck her head in, an apologetic half-smile on her face. "I heard the ruckus. Need a break?"

Sheriff Marge handed Jesamie over, and Hallie backed out of the room, pulling the door closed behind her, dampening Jesamie's complaints. After five years of marriage to Sheriff Marge's middle son, Hallie must know how to read the Stettler body language for official business. I'd noticed Ben Stettler adopting the same stiff stance, legs spread wide and arms crossed, earlier in the evening. It was the default pose for both mother and son—they were always in work mode.

"Can you e-mail the image?" Sheriff Marge asked. "I'll send it to neighboring law enforcement agencies and the FBI. They track stolen art."

Rupert snorted. "It's a piece of crap, not art."

"But whoever singled it out must have a reason for doing so," I said. "Or maybe there are others—" I didn't want to finish. "I also think someone broke into my office. They must have picked the lock, because there's no damage to the handle or door frame. As far as I can tell, they didn't disturb anything inside."

Sheriff Marge gave a curt nod. "I know it's crowded, but take a walk-through. See if anything else is missing, any of your more valuable pieces. I'll send Dale up to dust your office for prints." Sheriff Marge removed her reading glasses and pinched the bridge of her nose. "He might as well check yours, too, Rupert. I take it you haven't been up there this evening?"

Rupert shook his head wearily. "Much as I would have liked to hibernate, my duties were as a host tonight."

I'd seen Deputy Dale Larson and his wife, Sandy, in the dessert line earlier. It was a special occasion for them, one of their rare chances to get out as a couple without their kids. I hated to interrupt their date.

Pete slid his hand under my elbow and gave it a gentle squeeze. "I'll go with you."

I'd already walked the majority of the museum's rooms with Jesamie, but now that the demonstrations were over, all the guests were inside, meandering through the building and creating a human obstacle course. Some of our rarest, and most valuable, items are small and tucked away in secure display cases scattered throughout the exhibits. It's not like we lump them all together and label them with a big sign that reads, "Look here—the most expensive stuff." A thief would have to scope the joint first and know exactly what he was looking for to make the burglary profitable.

Pete ran interference for me, stopping to chat here and there with friends, some of whom had come great distances to lend their support. I waved, tried to appear cheerful, and accepted congratulations on the success of the event and condition of the museum—all the while darting nervous glances at the display cases, ticking items off the checklist in my head.

In spite of Pete's efforts, Barbara Segreti, proprietress of the Golden Shears Salon, cornered me near the velvet rope that blocked access to the basement stairs.

"How is everything?" She stretched out a plump hand encased in a lace glove and patted my brown curls, which were miraculously still in the elaborate pinned-up style she'd orchestrated. "Holding up?"

I'm not too comfortable being primped in public, and I tried to dodge her touch without offending her. "Perfect. Thanks. Lots of compliments."

"Good." Barbara sighed and clasped her hands in front of her. She was dressed in a flowing empire-waist gown that flattered her short, round form, giving her some definition. She looked worried.

She'd probably cut, dyed, highlighted, lowlighted, straightened, curled, or arranged the hair of half the ladies in attendance sometime in the past few days. Maybe the thought of so much of her handiwork on display made her nervous.

"Are you having a good time?" I asked.

"Of course, hon." But Barbara's eyes drifted across the ballroom. "Is Rupert here? I haven't seen him."

"I know—it's so crowded. Try the buffet lines. He's bound to show up there sooner or later."

"Right." Barbara nodded, her lips pressed in a thin, bright-fuchsia-lipsticked line. She bustled off.

I completed the tour in the photograph archive room on the second floor. Pete and I were alone because dusty cabinets stuffed with curling sepia prints and brittle negatives aren't particularly appealing to visitors unless they're doing specific research. I checked the last drawer of glass slides for railroad publicity photos of the Columbia River Gorge. They're not valuable even though there are very few left. But they're some of my favorites, so I scanned them anyway.

"Well?" Pete asked.

I turned to him and sighed. "Looks good. I might have missed something, with all the people—" I bit my lip.

Pete wrapped me in a tight hug, then backed off a little. "Babe, you're crusty."

"Oh." I brushed at the snail trails on my shoulders and dress bodice. "Jesamie residue. But it all came out her top end, so it's okay."

Pete chuckled and pulled me close again. "You're worried about something more. What?"

"I never had the painting x-rayed. Maybe I should have," I murmured into his chest.

Pete tipped my chin up. "Why?" His brows drew together. "It was repulsive—and I like fishing."

I couldn't help smirking. I'd forgotten he'd seen the painting. "Exactly. There's no reason for anyone to steal it unless—" I picked at one of the pearl studs in his shirt.

"Unless?"

I took a deep breath. "I have a horrible feeling good ol' Cosmo might have painted over something that really is valuable—either as a joke or as a way to protect what's underneath." I gritted my teeth. "It didn't occur to me until someone else decided the painting was worth stealing."

"What can you do now?"

"There are some canvas bits still pinched in the frame. I can have the paint on them analyzed. Maybe the pigments are different ages or different types that might indicate multiple layers."

ooo

It took a couple more hours for the museum to empty out. The guests seemed reluctant to return to real life. Frankie offered to stay and lock up after the catering crew, so I kissed Pete goodnight, drove to my fifth-wheel trailer, fed my hound Tuppence, stripped off my gown, and flopped into bed without bothering to wash my face or brush my teeth.

But as I lay there in the dark, my brain went into overdrive. Why was such a personal item taken? A Hagg family piece. Was it revenge or a vendetta of some kind? I couldn't shake the idea that whoever stole the painting knew the family's history.

Tomorrow, I would need to take an accounting of the collections in the basement. I was slowly working through the backlog down there, and most of it hadn't been documented yet. There'd be no way other than a visual inspection to know if anything had been stolen from among the boxes and crates piled in the cavernous room, which ran almost the entire length of the old mansion.

I also kept coming back to the hunch that the painting must have been stolen during normal visiting hours, if not that night. The only reason I could see for cutting the canvas from the frame was to be able to roll up the painting in order to sneak it out of the building. Still, a tube 54 inches long would be noticeable. I flipped through my mental images of the evening, trying to remember if I'd seen anyone with such a bulky package. It's hard to hide something that long when you're wearing black tie. Since it was late summer, no trench coats had been in attendance.

The catering crew might have had opportunity—and large equipment that could be used to conceal the painting. But they were all ladies I knew—or at least I recognized their husbands. Finney had recruited the wives of some of his regular customers at the Burger Basket & Bait Shop, retired men who fished from the marina boardwalks and shot the breeze daily with their cronies. The ladies were a sweet bunch and had been so excited about the opportunity when I checked on them a few minutes before we opened the doors. They'd done a great job of applying motherly pressure to make sure the guests sampled Finney's approximation of cowboy fare: five-bean chili, blue-cheese corncakes, sweet-potato fries, grilled veggie kabobs, and best of all, apple fritters and peach turnovers. Finney is indeed a master of the deep-fat fryer.

An hour later, I was still wide-awake and stewing. My phone rang, loud against the white noise of the campground's sprinkler system cycling through its nightly rotation. I rolled over, checked the red clock numbers—2:12 a.m.—and grabbed the phone.

"Yeah?" I grunted.

"Meredith?" A timid female voice. "It's Hallie Stettler. Mom's been in an accident. She's at the hospital in Lupine. I just thought—maybe—would you come? I got your number from her phone."

"Sheriff Marge?" I leaped out of bed, my heart pounding. "Is she okay? How bad is it?"

"I don't know yet. We just got here." Hallie sounded close to tears, and I heard Jesamie wailing in the background.

"Twenty minutes, tops." I hopped around, trying to pull on a pair of shorts one-handed. "I'm coming."

CHAPTER 3

I raced along a deserted State Route 14 and careened into the hospital's parking lot. I sprinted to the double sliding glass doors of the emergency room entrance.

Hallie waited just inside, bouncing a screaming Jesamie on her hip. "Could you take her, please? The doctor wants to speak with us, but—"

"Sure." I scooped the baby against my chest and cuddled her.

Hallie shot me a distracted half-smile and hurried toward a curtained-off side room. My stomach knotted tight around my worry, but I turned to the teary and distraught matter at hand.

Drawing on my wealth of experience from the fundraiser, I paced with Jesamie in the empty waiting room, humming to her. Poor kid. Maybe she had colic. Her sleep schedule must have gone haywire with the plane trip out here, staying in a new place, being jostled through a crowded event, then dashing to the hospital in the middle of the night—not to mention meeting her grandmother for the first time.

I've always loved kids, as long as they're somebody else's. The biological clock—the burning desire for motherhood—that other women talk about is notably absent in my case. I'd rather plan a fun craft or science project and then play with the kids and send them home when they're tired, which is why the museum has several hands-on exhibits designed especially for children and the young at heart.

A soft hand squeezed my arm, and I turned. Gemma. I sighed with relief.

Gemma's the nurse who took such good care of my friend George a few weeks ago—saved his life, really. She's one of those take-charge people who boss you around and you come away grateful for the instruction.

"Let me." She gestured for me to hand over the sobbing Jesamie. "You watch football?"

I nodded.

"Hold her like this." Gemma demonstrated a tight football tuck with her right arm, the way coaches wish wide receivers and running backs would cradle the ball and quit showboating.

Jesamie gurgled and calmed into jerky sighs. Just like that, her little body relaxed.

Gemma blinked at me with giant, pale-green eyes behind burgundy-framed cat's-eye glasses. "Snug. So she knows you're there but has room to wriggle. Helps the gas pass. Think you can do it?"

"You're amazing." I stretched my arms to assume the correct hold on Jesamie.

"I'm old. I've done this too many times to count."

"What do you know about Sheriff Marge? Can you tell me?"

Gemma pursed her lips for a moment, then nodded. "You're close enough to family. It'll be all over the county later this morning anyway. Wrapped her Explorer around a tree."

I groaned. Sheriff Marge always drives fast, as though every moment of her life is an emergency. Given her job and how thinly stretched she and her deputies are, most of the time that's true.

"Whole left side's banged up. Broken femur, for sure, maybe broken arm bones. Back pain. Doc just got the X-rays, and he's discussing treatment with her son and daughter-in-law while the OR nurses are prepping Sheriff Marge for surgery."

"This won't be"—I gulped a breath—"career-ending, will it?"

Gemma snorted. "Sheriff Marge? Not likely. But the recuperation time—kick in the pants, that'll be. She'll need someone at home to help care for her."

Jesamie was drooling on my arm. I massaged her back with my free hand, frowning. "Maybe we can do it in shifts."

The scooped ends of Gemma's shellacked bouffant bobbed. "She's gonna get cranky, being cooped up."

I frowned. "No kidding."

"Meredith. Gemma." Deputy Dale Larson hurried up. "How is she?"

"She'll live," Gemma said.

"Well, I figured that, given the way she was ranting about the Lamborghini driver." Dale shook his head with a wry grin. "Whooo."

"What happened?" I asked.

"She finally got a bead on the phantom Lamborghini. He's been on WSP's radar the past few weeks, hitting speeds near 200 mph, always after dark, but no one's caught him yet. She missed a curve on State Route 14 near the Benton County line. Her SUV's in chunks. Verle had to bring his flatbed tow truck out to pick up the pieces."

Dale ran a hand through his short hair and exhaled. "She's really okay?"

"I'm pretty sure all her broken parts are fixable." Gemma patted his arm. "But she'll need time to mend."

Dale sank into a mustard-yellow, vinyl-coated waiting-room chair and stretched his legs out, nodding. He scrubbed a hand over his 3:00 a.m. beard shadow and exhaled again. "Okay. Ben and Hallie know?"

I rocked Jesamie in his direction.

"Right. Man, I'm exhausted. You just don't expect to have to respond to the scene of your boss's wreck, you know?" Dale shook his head.

I perched on the edge of the chair beside him and eased Jesamie onto my lap. Her tiny, wet eyelashes rested on pink cheeks. She gave a shuddery sigh but didn't wake.

"Peaceful," Dale said. "At least someone around here gets to sleep."

"It'll be hours," Gemma said. "You all could go home."

Dale and I glanced at each other. His brown eyes were bloodshot and red-rimmed, but unwavering.

"We're staying," I said.

"Thought so. I'll see about coffee." Gemma's stiff uniform swished as she strode away.

"Since you're here and I'm here, how 'bout some fingerprints?" Dale asked. "I need to take yours so I can eliminate them from the prints I lifted in your office today." His brows drew together and he frowned. "Yesterday."

I nodded.

Dale retrieved the kit from his cruiser. Ben and Hallie joined us, silent and worried.

Once Dale had captured my fingerprints with the digital scanner, I slouched in the chair and tucked Jesamie's fuzzy head under my chin, her soft little body snuggled against mine. Hallie was too preoccupied to ask for her back, and I didn't want to relinquish the infant anyway. She was solid and warm and comforting to hold on to while I waited.

ooo

I ended up getting home after daybreak. Sheriff Marge's surgery went better than the doctor expected, with both breaks in her femur clean but still needing pins. Her elbow turned out to be sprained, not broken as originally feared. She was going to be sore for a very long time.

I'd been allowed to slip into her room for a moment, to confirm to my satisfaction that she really was alive. She'd grunted and opened one gray eye for a second when I'd squeezed her hand. It would have to do, for now.

I unlocked the fifth-wheel, trudged up the steps, and dumped my purse on the kitchen table. I stared, blurry-eyed and groggy, at the coffeemaker. There was no point in going to bed. Not considering what I needed to accomplish today.

Tuppence whined and stretched on her big pillow bed, then tucked her nose back under her haunch and resumed snoring.

I poked the coffeemaker's start button and stumbled into the bathroom. Maybe a cold shower would jolt me to full consciousness.

It did—for about ten minutes. As I pulled on a work-appropriate blouse and skirt, my numbness returned. It was going to be a multi-espresso day.

The Imogene felt like a ghost mansion when I unlocked the front doors and stepped through them, insulated coffee mug in hand. Crumpled paper napkins had been swirled into the ballroom's corners by the whoosh of long-skirted evening gowns. Corncake crumbs and dropped sweet-potato fries lay squashed on the floor. The stale air still smelled of chili.

The Imogene's seen her share of parties. I wondered if the next day always carried this sense of abandonment even when the mansion served as the Hagg family's vacation home.

"Don't worry about the mess." Frankie breezed in behind me. "I arranged for a double cleaning crew today."

I sighed and turned to her.

Frankie stopped in her tracks, her dimple disappearing. "What happened to you?"

Where to start? I explained about Sheriff Marge's collision.

Frankie's hand fluttered to her mouth.

"She'll be okay, eventually." I rubbed my forehead. "But there's something else. You know Cosmo Hagg's still life of a salmon and fishing gear on the third floor?"

Frankie's face puckered in distaste. "Yes?"

"When was the last time you saw it?"

"Oh. Gosh, I don't know. It's just there."

"Not anymore."

Frankie clutched the pendant on her necklace, frowning. "What do you mean?"

"It was stolen sometime in the past few days, cut from the frame."

Frankie yanked on the hem of her emerald-green jacket and bit her lips. Her face flushed. A giggle escaped. Then peals of laughter. Her brown helmet hair vibrated.

I scowled. Were Sheriff Marge and I the only ones taking the theft seriously? Then I remembered that Sheriff Marge hadn't seen the painting. Everyone who knew the painting was exhibiting extreme glee at its disappearance—except me.

"Oh dear," Frankie wheezed. "I suppose that's bad?"

"I need to inventory the rest of our exhibits and undocumented items today to see if anything else was stolen."

"Oh." Frankie's brows arched, and her smile went slack. "What can I do to help?"

"For one, let's keep this confidential. I don't want our lack of security advertised. And I'll finish sooner if I'm not interrupted."

Frankie nodded. "I'll hold your calls, sign for any deliveries, and keep visitors out of your way."

I expelled a big breath. "Sorry. I don't mean to be grouchy. I suppose there's a chance the painting's been stashed somewhere in the building. It's probably been rolled into a tube, 54 inches long. Did you see any of our guests with something that size last night?"

"No. But I'll check every inch of the main floor today." Frankie patted my arm, worry wrinkles creasing her forehead. "Maybe it's just a prank."

I started in the basement and chided myself for not having taken pictures of the piles of boxes and crates—to have at least some kind of
record of what's down there. Better late than never, I flipped on every
light switch and snapped a series of frames with our digital camera for
a panoramic view of the Imogene's storage area.

Then I grabbed our heavy-duty emergency flashlight and walked
slowly down the center aisle, using the extra illumination to scan the
front edges and check between each stack of boxes for disturbance in
the dust on the concrete floor.

Nothing appeared to have been rearranged or removed. I closed my
eyes and mentally reviewed the topography of the room, then opened
my eyes to see if what was in front of me matched what I remembered.
It did—all of it.

I checked the basement's exterior door—locked.

I scowled, fists on hips, and exhaled. Like everyone else, I would
have given away Cosmo's painting if I could have. But what bothered
me was the intrusion, the stealth of the act, and the violation of my
bucolic world. The Imogene is *my* museum—as much as it can be for
anyone not named Hagg, anyway. And the theft was just—I struggled
for words—mean. Some joke—unless it was used to mask a greater
theft. The thought made my stomach plunge.

I trudged upstairs to my office, where I pulled up the museum's
collection database and printed it. Starting on the third floor, I worked
from room to room and floor to floor, glad to be on my feet. I had to
keep moving or my brain would shut down from lack of sleep.

Fortunately, I have counts per collection. So if the printout said
we had nineteen Klickitat beaded pouches, and nineteen beaded items
were in the display case, I checked the whole collection off. I'd go into
a detailed item-by-item review if one of the collections turned up short.

But none did.

So either the thief hadn't stolen anything other than the painting,
or he'd swapped counterfeit items for real artifacts. But that level of

preparation and deception didn't pair well with hacking a canvas out of a frame. What did Sheriff Marge call it—MO? Modus operandi.

I plunked cross-legged on the floor in the petroglyph room and reviewed the checklist.

"Meredith?" Frankie's voice echoed in the hallway.

"In here," I hollered.

Frankie's head appeared in the doorway. "You okay?"

I stretched my legs out and dropped the printout between them. "Just taking a break." I pressed my hands behind my neck and arched my back to stretch out the kinks.

"I know I said I'd hold your calls." Frankie moved into the room. She was clutching the gift shop's cordless phone against her thigh, her palm over the speaker holes. "But it's your mother. She sounds upset. She said she's been trying your cell phone all day, and you haven't been answering. So she called the museum number."

My jaw dropped. My mother never calls me—and I'm not exaggerating. I call her on her birthday and Mother's Day. For my birthday, I get a card in the mail with a couple folded twenties. She signs her name but never adds to the sappy sentiments that are printed on the card.

"Meredith?" Frankie squeaked, her brows pinched together. "Are you sure you're okay?"

"Yeah." I scrabbled to my feet. "Um, thanks." I reached for the phone and pressed it to my ear, turning away from Frankie.

"Hello?"

"Meredith? Where have you been?" Mom's voice had that edge to it—the one that makes me rapidly scan my recent history to figure out what I've been doing wrong.

I frowned. "Working."

"Well, I'm twenty minutes away, if this GPS thing can be trusted. I'm in no condition to see your museum today. I'll wait at your"—she sniffed—"your modular home." She hung up.

24

I thrust the phone to arm's length and stared at it like it was an alien life form.

"Meredith?" Frankie piped up behind me. She gingerly took the phone from my grasp. "I'm being nosy, but you and your mother don't really speak, do you? Are you okay, hon?" She reached up and squeezed my shoulder.

I gazed into Frankie's warm brown eyes and opened my mouth, but nothing came out.

Frankie nodded encouragingly, her earrings glinting.

"Where am I going to put her?" I croaked. "What time is it? She'd never deign to actually sleep in my trailer." I groaned and covered my eyes.

"It's almost six o'clock," Frankie said. "I take it your mother's coming to visit?"

"Why?" I stared at Frankie again. "She makes reservations weeks in advance for lunch at her favorite restaurant. But with me she just shows up?"

"She did say she'd been trying to call you all day."

I blew out a big, shuddering breath.

"There, there." Frankie wrapped an arm around my waist and propelled me out of the room. "Is this the first time she's visited you here?"

I nodded. "She thinks I'm crazy. This lifestyle—" I waved my hands. "When I could have had so much more—more money and things, I mean—if I'd stayed in Vancouver with my job in Portland. She doesn't understand, doesn't appreciate—freedom."

"Most don't," Frankie said with a side hug. "Until they've experienced it for themselves. I'll lock up. You'd better go." She gave me a little shove toward the grand staircase.

When I reached the bottom step, she called out, "Oh, uh, is anything else missing, besides the painting?"

I curled the checklist into a tube and tapped it against my palm. "No, nothing obvious."

Frankie nodded. "I'll still keep my eyes open."

CHAPTER 4

I pulled into the Riverview RV Ranch and wound around the loops to my fifth-wheel trailer. Tuppence scrambled to greet me, but didn't have time to run her cold nose over my shins as I flung open the trailer door and dashed up the steps.

I do not live in the manner to which my mother is accustomed, or in a manner to which she would *like* to become accustomed. She's acutely aware of distinctions, as most social climbers are. By moving to the boonies and taking a job at a decrepit nonprofit cultural institution, I've opened up new realms of distinctions that my mother can't even fathom.

Once, straight out of high school, she stepped out of her family's designated path to prominence and married my father. Alex, the man her family wished she'd married first, swooped in to rescue us when I was four, shortly after my father was found deceased under questionable circumstances—that's the family's polite way of saying drug overdose—in a third-world country. He'd been missing for a while. Alex is a lawyer, and he made some of the ugliness of that situation disappear quietly.

However, I'm the living reminder of my mother's earlier indiscretion, and that makes things pretty awkward for the three of us. As a stepfather, Alex is gracious in a stiff, unforgiving sort of way, but he provided generously when I was growing up. He probably still would, if I asked, but I've been way beyond asking for a long time now.

I keep things tidy. It's a necessity when you live in such a cramped space, so there wasn't much I could do to spruce up the place. I plumped couch cushions and tucked a few stray papers and books back onto the shelves. I dumped the leftover coffee from this morning and washed the pot. I kept tripping over Tuppence, who was obviously confused by my flurry.

"Sorry, old girl. I guess we'll be bunkmates for a while." I tousled her ears. Tuppence snores like the dickens, which is why she usually sleeps in the living room while I keep the bedroom to myself.

The purr of a large, sophisticated motor pulled up outside and went quiet. I squeezed my eyes shut and took a deep breath. A car door opened and thudded closed. High heels clacked on the asphalt driveway.

I pushed open the trailer door and stuck my head out. "Mom."

"Meredith." Mom wobbled a bit on her heels and fluttered an unconvincing smile. Her hazel eyes were red-rimmed, the lashes stuck together with clumped mascara.

"What's wrong?" I slowly descended the steps.

Mom shrugged and glanced away. "Oh—I decided to take a drive." She flicked a wrist toward the Columbia River, which runs behind my campsite, her French manicure glinting. "It's a beautiful day."

I might have forgotten to mention that my mother is gorgeous, even when in distress. Which she clearly was, although I might be the only person who'd recognize the cracks in the veneer. She wore a peach silk blouse tucked into slim white jeans. Her shoulder-length auburn hair was pulled back in an attractively messy chignon. She'd been driving with the Mercedes's windows down. Most of her makeup had been wiped off along with her tears, revealing her smooth skin. Always put on a good face, even for your closest relatives—it was a mantra the entire family lived by, so deeply ingrained as to be impenetrable.

I sighed. "Right. You hungry? I'm just fixing dinner."

Mom smiled again, a little stronger this time. "I'll keep you company."

I led Mom into the trailer and pointed to the chairs crowded around the dining table. "Have a seat." I ducked behind the kitchen island and pulled out a loaf of sourdough, a hunk of Muenster, and a container of dried cranberries.

But Mom paced to the fireplace at the end of the trailer and gazed out the big picture window above it. Tuppence trailed after her and inspected the white jeans from the knees down.

Mom trilled a little laugh and cupped the hound's head in her hands. "You must be Tuppence."

Tuppence thumped her tail on the floor in agreement.

I flopped two cheese sandwiches on the grill and scowled.

"So you really live here—year-round?"

I gulped a breath. Another ritual—asking questions she already knows the answers to—safe territory. "Yes."

"You're comfortable?"

"Yes."

"Even in winter?"

"Yes."

Mom sighed. "It's lovely."

I almost dropped the spatula. She approved? I glanced at her, but she was staring out the window.

I decided to try a different tactic. "How's Alex?"

Mom didn't turn, but her hands clenched at her sides. "Working."

Alex is always working. It's his greatest trait. "Did you have a fight?"

Mom spun around, her face about to crumble, but she pulled it into a tight smile at the last moment. "Just a difference of opinion. I needed a few days away."

I nodded slowly, trying to see behind the flat look in her eyes. "I have some stuff going on at the museum, so I won't be able to take time off."

"No need," Mom said quickly. "I don't want to be a bother."

I carried our plates outside to the picnic table. The RV was still a little stuffy from being closed up all day. We sat side by side on the north side of the table in order to enjoy the view of the river and the hazy Oregon bank opposite.

Mom gingerly picked up the warm, oozy slab and bit into the sandwich. "Mmm."

I bit in, too.

Mom wiped a cheese string from her chin. "You always were a good cook, even as a child. I'd turn you loose with the *Betty Crocker Cookbook*. Remember?"

"I remember melting a Tupperware container all over the electric burner."

Mom laughed and popped an errant cranberry in her mouth.

Something was going on. Mom and Alex fought regularly all through my childhood, but never, to my knowledge, had either of them left. She wasn't going to tell me—not now, maybe not ever. What could I do?

"I have a problem at the museum," I blurted.

Mom's perfectly sculpted brows arched.

"A theft. We're trying to keep it from becoming public knowledge until we figure out who and why." I shook my head. "It's unusual. Maybe—based on your experience as an art therapist—maybe you'd have some insight?"

Mom set down her sandwich, a little spark lightening her eyes. "Yes. Of course. I mean—I don't know what I could do—but I'll try."

I breathed a sigh of relief—it was the perfect distraction, a way to keep her busy. "I forgot to e-mail the image to law enforcement earlier today. So how about we go to the Imogene as soon as we're finished eating? I'll fill you in there."

ooo

I pushed open the door to my office and flipped the lights on. The doorknob, desk, and bookshelf surfaces were still smeary from Dale's fingerprint dust.

"Careful what you touch," I said, eyeing Mom's white jeans. "It's a little dirty in here."

I fired up the laptop and shoved some papers out of the way.

Mom sidestepped around piles on the floor and moved to the big picture window. "All these views," she breathed.

The late summer sun was just setting at the unseen mouth of the Columbia, making the river look like liquid gold between flanking hills gradating from green to cobalt to violet-tinged black.

"Are sunsets here always this breathtaking?" she asked over her shoulder.

I grinned. "All the time. Take a look at this." I turned the laptop so she could see the screen.

Mom gasped.

"Yeah." I dropped into my chair. "And someone stole it."

Mom hinged at the waist and leaned forward, peering at the image of the still life. She traced the major elements in the image with her finger. "It's terrible."

"That's the consensus," I said.

Mom cocked her head, still intent on the screen. "Even small children have an innate sense of balance and symmetry. Maybe not proportion, but they'll fill a whole page with motifs. This—" she shook her head. "This was done by an adult trying way too hard. Trying to make a statement."

I sat up straight. "What kind of statement?"

Mom shrugged. "I don't know. I'd have to watch the person over a series of sessions, see how he interacts with the medium, read his body language. Is the artist—"

"Dead," I said. "About forty years ago."

Mom squinted and leaned closer. "Is it three-dimensional?"

"I'm not sure if it was an artistic technique or a series of accidents—you know, the 'I don't like how that turned out, so I'll just add a little bit more' method over and over—the opposite of the way bad haircuts happen. So, yes—very thick acrylics, decoupage, and some real items, like fishing line, glued on top."

Mom wrinkled her nose. "When was it painted?"

I clicked open the painting's description. "It's not dated, but it was donated to the museum in 1973, along with $85,000. Here it is—Cosmopolitan Humphrey Hagg, born 1922 in Orange County, California. Died April 13, 1974, in Astoria, Oregon, in a boating accident. I'm not sure how he was related to Rupert. Here's a scan of his obituary with a picture."

A bald, jowly man with thick glasses and hooded eyes gazed stoically from the screen in a black-and-white head shot.

"A real firecracker." Mom giggled. "Who names their son Cosmopolitan?"

"Eccentricity runs in the family." I attached the painting image and description to an e-mail. I addressed the note to Sheriff Marge and Dale since I wasn't sure who'd be handling the case with Sheriff Marge laid up. I also fired off a copy with a slightly different note to a forensic art investigator I know by reputation.

I checked my watch. "I'd like to visit a friend in the hospital. Do you want to settle in at the trailer? I'll drop you off."

"No—I mean, yes. I'll get situated later. The couch will suit me fine, by the way. But I'd like to meet your friends, if that's okay?" A little furrow appeared between Mom's brows.

It suddenly hit me just how out of her element she was. While only a few hours separate Platts Landing from Vancouver, the culture is vastly different—and even more foreign for someone like my mother. I had no idea why she would voluntarily visit. I also got the impression she didn't want to be left alone. Something was definitely going on.

"Sure." I smiled.

As we drove to the hospital, I told Mom how I'd found the painting missing, cut from the frame, and how I needed to have the fragments analyzed for different paint types or ages.

"If the thief knows something I don't—if there's a valuable painting underneath the mess Cosmo added, then why did he cut it out?" I said.

Most of the fine art stolen around the globe is small, easily carried by a single person. The thieves just don't bother with bigger works because they don't have the time to properly remove the painting from the frame, and everyone knows that cutting it out slashes its value— both at auction and on the street. There have been a few instances of cutting out Old Masters, but the speculation is that the thieves were working for an obsessive private collector and that those paintings would never reemerge on any market, black or legitimate. The damage to the painting was the price the collector was willing to pay to possess the art.

"Maybe it has nothing to do with art," Mom said. "Maybe it's personal."

I gripped the steering wheel tighter. "That's what I'm thinking, too, and it scares me more."

Mom's voice was muffled, strained. "You love this place, the museum, don't you?"

I couldn't see her face in the dark. "Yes," I whispered. I hoped she didn't think it meant I loved her less. Just different. But how do you say that?

CHAPTER 5

Sheriff Marge lay stiff and swaddled, propped in an elevated bed. She looked naked and shrunken without her Stratton hat, and the white hospital gown with little blue dots did nothing for her complexion—she was made to wear khaki. Her short salt-and-pepper hair stuck up in back—pillow styling. Dale was stretched out between two visitors' chairs—his behind in one, and his ankles crossed on the seat of the other. He had his notebook out, as though he was reporting on the day's activities.

A quick glance around the room showed it had been transformed into "Operations Central"—computer printouts covered the rolling bedside table. A handheld walkie-talkie quietly garbled static from its place on the blankets near Sheriff Marge's right hand. A laptop was plugged into an outlet next to the IV stand.

"You look like you're feeling better," I said.

Sheriff Marge grunted, then quirked a brow above her reading glasses as Mom stepped into the room behind me.

Dale jumped to his feet and hastily brushed off the chair his boots had been on. "Howdy." He stuck out a hand. "You have to be Meredith's mom." His eyes darted from Mom to me. "Or sister."

Mom flushed and shook his hand. "Call me Pamela. Please."

Out of the corner of my eye, I caught Sheriff Marge glaring at me. Of all the people in Platts Landing—other than Pete—she knows the most about my desire for separation from my family. It was her "What's going on here?" glare.

I clamped a smile on my face. "I just e-mailed the painting image and description."

"Got it," Dale said. "Already forwarded it to the FBI, state, border patrol, and PDs in Seattle, Portland, Sacramento, San Francisco, and LA. It'll have to move through a major city if it's going to be sold."

"We gotta put a dollar value on it," Sheriff Marge said.

"I'll know more when the paint chips have been analyzed." I sighed. "Let's start with half a million."

Dale snorted. "Seriously?"

"It's not insured and has never been appraised, so I'm guessing—optimistically. But the bigger the number, the more law enforcement will be on the lookout, right? And maybe the thief'll stash it if he thinks it's too hot to sell right now—keep it from getting too far away?"

He whistled softly. "I suppose. Fingerprints were a bust, by the way. All yours."

"And in Rupert's office?"

"Yours and his—what I could collect. The place is a pigsty, and he wouldn't let me dust most of it—sensitive surfaces, he said."

I chuckled. Rupert's office is a disheveled museum unto itself, with his own personal collections and artifacts strewn in disarray. He's threatened to donate everything to the Imogene, and I dread the day I have to categorize his precious mementos while he hovers over my shoulder.

"Nothing else is missing from the museum. What can I do to help?" I asked.

"Notify us immediately if you receive any communication from the thief, or from anyone else about the painting. They might try blackmail. Many museums are willing to buy back their own art in order to protect it—a form of ransom—and to avoid negative publicity." Sheriff Marge shifted her rigid leg under the blankets, grimacing. "Does the Imogene have a fund for the retrieval of artwork, in lieu of insurance? Do you want to offer a reward?"

My mouth hung open for a second, then I snapped it closed, shaking my head. "We really don't. Nothing designated, anyway. I think the fundraiser went well. Frankie was doing a tally today, but I didn't hear the final number. But that money is supposed to be used for much-needed maintenance on the mansion. I need to talk to Rupert—maybe the board of directors could scrape up a little for a reward."

Sheriff Marge nodded. "We'll just sit tight for a bit, see what comes up in the channels, keep our eyes open."

"You never know. Maybe the thief forgot to renew his vehicle tabs and he's getting pulled over right now, with the painting in the backseat." Dale grinned. "Stupid stuff like that trips up criminals all the time."

I bit my lip. I was pretty sure *this* criminal was more organized and intelligent than Dale suggested. Mainly because he knew something I didn't—and it was driving me crazy.

"So you're here for a visit?" Sheriff Marge aimed her question at Mom.

Mom nodded. "Meredith always speaks of Platts Landing and the people here in such glowing terms I decided to come see for myself."

I ducked my head as I winced, hoping Mom wouldn't see. She was laying the charm on too thick. That kind of syrupy comment would never fly with Sheriff Marge, or Dale, or any of my other friends. Never mind that I wasn't sure her statement was quite true since we rarely spoke to each other about anything meaningful.

"Huh." Sheriff Marge folded her arms across her chest. "How long are you staying?"

Mom's smile wavered. "Um, a few days?" She darted a glance at me.

I pushed off the wall where I'd been leaning. "I guess we should get going."

"Me, too." Dale plunked his hat on his head. "See you in the mornin'." He nodded to Sheriff Marge.

"Huh." Sheriff Marge scowled and watched us exit the room single file.

As we walked down the squeaky waxed-linoleum hallway, I laid a hand on Dale's arm. "How is she—really?"

His cheeks puffed in a prolonged exhale. "This is not going to be pretty. I think she's about reached the limit of tolerating being bed-bound, and it's not even been twenty-four hours. You saw the equipment we brought in to keep her connected."

"So the pain must not be too bad—if she has the energy to be grouchy?"

Dale chuckled. "I suppose. She's sure not comfortable, though—shifts her leg around and adjusts the bed position every few minutes. The sooner she gets released, the better, even if it means she's barking orders from a recliner down at the station."

"Did the doctor say when?" The hospital's sliding glass doors whooshed open, and we stepped outside.

Dale angled toward his cruiser, which was parked at the end of the ambulance unloading zone. "Couple days. Ben has to get back to work in Chicago, but Hallie and the baby are staying for a week or two to help Sheriff Marge at home."

I waved and headed for my pickup, Mom at my heels. Maybe this enforced downtime for Sheriff Marge would enable her to bond with her new granddaughter. I snickered at the bedtime stories Sheriff Marge could tell Jesamie. Good thing she was too young to understand them. Otherwise, the kid wouldn't be sleeping for a week.

ooo

Mom was notably silent on the drive back to the campground. Normally, she has the ability to fill lulls in conversation with easy chatter. She's a master at cocktail-party mingling. Maybe the difficulty was that I wasn't in a partying mood.

The truth is, I don't like who I am—or who I become—in my mother's presence. We don't bring out the best in each other. It's something I've finally acknowledged, although I don't have a solution.

We worked in tandem to pull out the hide-a-bed couch and fit it with sheets and blankets. I dragged Tuppence's big pillow bed up the short stairs to my bedroom and wedged it between the dresser and the end of my bed. I hoped I still had a pair of earplugs squirreled away in the medicine cabinet—I was going to need them.

Mom and I quickly separated to our opposite ends of the trailer. I shut the bedroom door and dropped onto the edge of the mattress. Tuppence padded over and laid her muzzle on my thigh.

I traced the black-and-white markings on her head with my fingers. Her eyes closed in dreamy contentment.

"What's going on?" I whispered.

Tuppence cocked one eye open and winked at me.

"Any suggestions?"

She yawned—a huge, tongue-curling, audible stretch—then ambled over to her bed and flopped on it with a sigh.

"Good idea." I quickly changed into pajamas and followed suit.

I was floating—comfortable and dark, hanging by a thread— over the abyss of sleep when my phone rang. I lurched upright, heart pounding.

"Ugh." Not again. I checked the clock—only 10:15 p.m. And the caller ID said Alex Stephenson, my stepfather.

"Hello?"

"Meredith, is your mother with you?"

I frowned. "Yes."

Alex groaned faintly, but I couldn't tell if it was from relief or frustration.

"Didn't she tell you?"

"Where else would she go? But I wanted to make sure." He paused—too long.

"Alex?"

"There are a lot of things your mother hasn't been telling me. I know she needs some time. Take care of her, will you?"

"Done."

"Thank you." He hung up.

Try sleeping after that. I sprawled on the bed, staring at the ceiling and wondering about the woman in the living room. We were never close, but how had she become so distant? Was it my fault, since I'd broken physical proximity by moving away from my hometown? I'd needed the change for my own sanity, but at what cost to my mother? I hadn't thought she cared, except for the impression it gave others.

ooo

I only know of one effective way to deal with an unsettled mind—physical activity. I rose early and assembled a lasagna. I didn't try terribly hard to be quiet, and Mom rolled off the couch shortly after the ground beef was browned. The whole RV smelled like onions.

"You can have the bathroom first," I said cheerily. "The service starts at ten o'clock." If Mom truly wanted to meet the local residents, then Sunday morning was a good time to find a bunch of them congregated at Platts Landing Bible Church.

I had decided not to mention Alex's call. If Mom wanted to pretend this was a spontaneous, friendly visit, then I'd play along—for now.

We worked around each other in the narrow space, eating breakfast and getting ourselves prepared for the day, speaking only when absolutely necessary. Mom was showing some signs of wear, with dark circles under her eyes that even concealer couldn't fully mask. I wondered how much she'd slept and what was weighing on her mind—or conscience.

But she artfully diverted attention away from her face with a stunning outfit that showed off her tanned legs—a floaty knee-length sundress topped with a cropped lace jacket and mile-high platform peep-toe espadrilles that revealed perfect cherry-red toenail polish. She must have had a pedicure somewhere along the way yesterday.

I had Mom move her Mercedes to a shady spot next to my campsite. Her sleek, shiny car seemed inappropriate for daily life and the frequent gravel roads in Sockeye County.

We climbed into my trusty old pickup, and I headed toward State Route 14.

Already people were standing in loose groups in the church's parking lot, enjoying the sunshine and catching up with friends. I slid out of the truck just as Pete roared into the spot next to mine. He rocked the motorcycle up onto its stand and removed his helmet.

"Babe." He grinned and swung off the bike. He wrapped an arm around my waist, pulling me in for a quick kiss.

Normally, his scent of licorice and Barbasol—not to mention his warm lips—would make me weak-kneed, but I felt a little awkward knowing my mother was gaping from the other side of the pickup.

I snuck a hand up to his chest and cleared enough space to whisper, "I need to talk to you."

"Good morning." Mom's voice was high and clear—and very close.

I flinched and turned. She was standing a couple of feet way, eyes narrowed at Pete.

"Um, this is my mother, Pamela," I muttered. "She arrived yesterday afternoon."

Pete's grip on my waist tightened, but he didn't hesitate. "Pamela, good to meet you."

"Is it?" She sighed. "Well, I'm here now. Shall we go inside?" She pivoted and marched toward the church's double-door entrance on those fantastic espadrilles.

Pete fixed me with a stern look, his blue eyes intense, one brow arched.

I swallowed, my throat dry. "No warning. No explanation. Just showed up," I whispered. "Please, please, please come for lunch. I need backup."

His mouth didn't smile, but his eyes did—flashing those crinkle-corners for me. "I think she's going to have *me* for lunch. But if you need me—"

"Do I ever." I touched his cheek. "I made a huge pan of lasagna. I'll try to keep it between you and her so she has something else to eat first."

CHAPTER 6

Mom perked up at the prospect of meeting a bunch of strangers—one of the ways we're vastly different. She received a warm welcome. Visitors in Platts Landing are few and far between, so they're gushed over when they do appear. Most people would probably find so much enthusiasm overwhelming, but Mom reveled in it.

She surprised me, too, by knowing the words to the first couple of verses of every hymn we sang. How could have I grown up with this woman and still be mystified by her? And when was she going to fill in the blanks?

After the service, Pastor Mort Levine and his wife, Sally, found us and introduced themselves to Mom.

"Pete." Mort pumped Pete's hand. "How long are you in town?"

"Just here for the weekend—for the fundraiser." Pete smiled at me. "Leaving in the morning for Arlington. They're unloading the remainder of last year's wheat harvest to make room for this year's. Looks to be a heavy crop."

"That's what I'm hearing, too." Mort nodded. "Which is much-needed good news. Out to Astoria with the load?"

"Yep. It's heading to China."

Mort shook his head. "International trade and how the goods move around still amazes me. We'll be praying for safe travels."

Sally beamed in agreement and patted Pete's arm.

"Appreciate it." Pete grinned.

In the pickup with the windows down, now that our hair didn't need to remain in place for church, I informed Mom that Pete would be joining us for lunch.

She scowled, staring straight forward. "How long have you known him?"

"Um, six—no, eight months—wait, I think around a year." I shrugged. "A while, anyway."

"What does he do for a living? I didn't understand about the load of wheat. Is he a farmer?"

"Tugboat owner and operator. He moves all kinds of loads up and down the Columbia-Snake River System."

Mom's lips pressed together in a thin line, and I knew what she was thinking—blue collar. My jaw tightened, and I felt my face flush. I hated those snap judgments she made about people based on their appearance or their jobs or the cars they drove—putting them into categories without really knowing them. I wanted to explain that Pete is the most patient, gentle, kind, caring, hardworking man I'd ever known, but I also knew it would be a fruitless attempt.

"What was that about a fundraiser?"

"Oh, uh—" I'd been expecting a disparaging remark about Pete. Fundraiser? Of course, that's much more in my mother's territory. "For the museum. Friday night. Black tie and chili." I giggled at the discrepancy, and yet the chili had certainly contributed to the success of the evening.

"You planned it?"

"Frankie and I did. Frankie'll be at the museum tomorrow, so you can meet her then. She's a sweetheart."

"How many attendees?"

"Frankie'll have the final count. I think between 350 and 400."

"Meredith." Mom's voice sounded choked. "Why didn't you tell me? I could've helped."

"Frankie's great at event planning. She handled all the details—" I glanced at Mom. She was close to tears, blinking rapidly, still staring straight ahead. "Um—it was pretty simple, really. It's kind of far for you—" I clamped my mouth shut. Whatever I said, it would be the wrong thing.

I checked the rearview mirror. Pete was still back there on his motorcycle, trailing us to the campground. I said a silent prayer of thanks and exhaled slowly. I'd never make it through the rest of the day with my mother without Pete's steadying presence.

ooo

We survived lunch—well, I did—barely. I could tell Pete was figuratively gritting his teeth throughout the ordeal. Mom was strained, her chatter not coming as effortlessly as usual, as she searched for innocuous topics.

She extracted some of Pete's history—the high school injury that negated a full-ride college football scholarship and his subsequent enlistment in the navy; saving every spare cent so he could buy his tug, the *Surely*, after fifteen years of service and an honorable discharge; building his business on word of mouth and a willingness to take the unusual or particularly challenging tow jobs.

Mom was deadpan throughout, question after question, as though she was clicking through an eligibility checklist. Pete's voice deepened with the tension, and I scooted closer to him, sliding a hand under the picnic table to rub his knee. I felt guilty that I was enjoying a few minutes of freedom from Mom's critical spotlight while she focused on him instead.

I was about to suggest dessert as a diversion when an enormous motor coach with California plates and towing a U-Haul trailer rumbled around the loop and stopped beyond a full hook-up site several spaces away. The driver rolled down his window, stuck his head out, and started creeping in reverse. I recognized the thick glasses and pointed nose of Melvin Sharpe, the filmmaker I'd met at the fundraiser.

The RV lurched and jerked as the brake lights flashed on and off, the coach swaying from side to side under the strain of making the turn. Except he didn't make the turn, and the U-Haul ended up with one wheel in the fire pit of the next campsite over.

Melvin and someone in the passenger seat hollered at each other, then the motor coach leaped forward and the U-Haul bumped out of the fire pit.

"Just give me a minute," Melvin shouted.

"You're going to ruin it," a female voice flung back.

I cringed. "Maybe we should have our pie inside. Backing up with such a big coach plus a trailer is hard. Having spectators is worse." I stacked our plates and stood.

A door on the far side of the coach slammed, and a pair of feet in red stilettos appeared in the gap between the bottom of the coach and the ground. "You can't do anything right," the passenger yelled.

And this coming from a woman who thought spiked high heels were appropriate for camping? Straight from Hollywood, that pair. With my nerves and patience already stretched taut, the woman who belonged to those shoes—and that screechy voice—was about to push me over the edge.

"À la mode?" I asked with forced cheerfulness and sped for the steps up to my fifth-wheel.

Typically, my fellow campers are practical and friendly, the kind of people you have instant rapport with. But not always. I wondered how long making a documentary would take and if I'd have to listen to my new neighbors bickering every evening until then.

Pete, carrying the lasagna pan and chuckling, climbed the steps behind me. Mom followed, looking over her shoulder as the coach slammed into reverse for another attempt.

I scooped ice cream over peach-pie slices, and we huddled around the dining table. RVs aren't particularly well insulated, so we could still hear yelling, but at least I couldn't pick out the insulting words anymore. Mom kept peeking out the window, as though fascinated by this inappropriate social behavior.

"His name's Melvin Sharpe. He was at the fundraiser Friday night. He's doing a documentary on locavore culture, and apparently he, or his writers, think Platts Landing is a forward-thinking community in that regard." I snickered. "The truth is, we just eat what there is. We're certainly not snobbish about food. Everyone figures that if you grow it, you'd better not waste it."

"This"—Pete gestured with his fork at the pie and spoke around a mouthful—"is great."

I grinned. "Windfalls." The campground is nestled in the remnants of old orchards—peach, pear, and apricot. The fruit is free for the taking, one of the perks for residents.

We scraped our plates clean in silence, and Pete helped me wash the dishes.

Mom stayed seated, gazing out the window and toying with her coffee mug until she finally said, "They're parked now and seem to be setting up. Should we go say hello?"

Pete raised his brows at me and shrugged.

I nodded in response to his unasked question. Mom feels most comfortable in the middle of a big group. This lazy Sunday afternoon was probably driving her crazy. "Sure."

We tromped across the intervening campsites and rounded the big coach. Melvin had his head stuck in a side compartment, and he was pounding on something.

Pete cleared his throat. "Need a hand with those jacks?"

Melvin peeked under his arm, squinting through the thick glasses. "Um, yeah, I guess not sure what—"

"Pete—baby!" A well-endowed blonde bombshell appeared in the coach's side door—she of the red stilettos. "What a surprise!" She flew down the stairs and flung her arms around Pete's neck, smacking him with a big, juicy kiss. She sort of missed—or maybe he flinched?—and she hit the corner of his mouth, leaving a lipstick streak on his cheek.

Pete took a step back, flushing dark.

The blonde hung on him, giggling. "Oh, you cutie. I haven't seen you in forever," she gushed.

I did not have the decency to stop staring and close my mouth. When sense returned—just a momentary lapse—I whirled, turning my back on the scene, my breathing fast and shallow. In a fraction of a second, I'd scoped all escape routes and identified the most promising one.

Mom materialized at my side and gripped my elbow with iron fingers. "Steady," she hissed.

"I'm leaving," I whispered.

"No, you're not." Mom gritted the words out in a barely audible voice, exhibiting amazing ventriloquism skills. She steered me back around to face the awkward group.

Melvin had also risen to his full height, and he was shuffling his feet, his Adam's apple bobbing fast.

Mom strode forward, straight up to Pete, who had his hands on the blonde's waist while she murmured into his neck. She stuck out her right hand. "Pamela Stephenson. So informative to meet you."

The blonde had to disentangle herself from Pete in order to shake Mom's hand. "Tiffany Reese. I love your shoes."

I was shuffling backward, doing my best to disappear. Where's an invisibility cloak when you need one? I felt as though I'd been kicked in the stomach. Maybe if I closed my eyes, what I was seeing would become a bad dream instead of reality—

I thudded into the front corner of the motor coach and slid around the headlight and grill, smearing bug guts on my blouse in the process. I leaned there, panting. Tuppence nudged my leg and wagged hopefully.

"You're right. The perfect time for a walk," I muttered.

Tuppence dropped in a play bow, her behind up in the air and tail swishing from side to side.

I set out at a fast clip, Tuppence trotting at my heels. I tried to stretch my hands out of the tight fists they'd clenched into. And I focused on breathing. In—out. In—out. It's just that this had happened before—different man, same predicament. And once was more than enough for me.

I never thought Pete would—I just never imagined—

I bit my lip, fighting back tears, and veered onto the riverside path. Tuppence clambered over the boulders lining the riverbank, poking her nose into the crevasses and snorting. Every once in a while she's rewarded with an indignant frog or worried furry creature, and that hope keeps her looking. I sniffed—life would be so much easier as a dog.

A big pile of rocks formed a short natural jetty just beyond the campground property. I climbed over them out to the tip, careless of my skirt and scraping my legs. I found a smooth spot on the promontory rock and perched on the edge, feet dangling over the water.

Normally, the river is a source of comfort for me, but I stared at the murky waves slapping the shore without seeing them. I was numb, and my brain slogged through the campground scene without making sense of anything. The only thing that stood out was the deadening feeling that I appeared to be following in my mother's footsteps—one miserable relationship after another.

I laid back. High cirrus clouds swirled—wispy feathers and fans—sifting like sand over a pale blue glass sea. Swirling, curling, dispersing.

I squeezed my eyes shut and pressed the heels of my palms into them. But it was no use—the memory of Pete holding the blonde was already permanently etched on my mind's screen. Tears ran into my ears.

OOO

"Meredith! For goodness' sake. Are you asleep?" Mom's irritated tone sounded close, almost as if she was speaking from inside my own head.

I sat up with a gasp, then scrunched my eyes closed and opened them again—in case I'd missed something. The world was still dark, filtered in gray scale from the fading dusk in the west end of the gorge, as though I'd regained consciousness in a different dimension. But that really was my mother's voice approaching.

"What are you doing?" A black form wobbled on the rock next to me, and she clutched my shoulder as she eased into a tenuous sitting position. "You had me worried."

"I guess I did fall asleep," I mumbled. "Still catching up from no sleep the other night—when Sheriff Marge had her accident."

"Still running," Mom said quietly.

I knew what she meant, but I wasn't in the mood to discuss my foibles. "So are you."

Mom sighed. "I know. You learned it from me." She grabbed my hand, jumped to her feet, and yanked me up as well. "Come on."

I teetered on the edge of the boulder, but Mom gave me another yank, and I stumbled forward, slipping and sliding as she pulled me toward shore. It was probably good I couldn't see where I was going, so I never knew how close I came to falling off the jetty.

My feet hit solid dirt and damp grass, then a cold nose bumped my knee.

"If it weren't for Tuppence, I still wouldn't know where you were," Mom snapped. "This has gone on long enough."

She dragged me along the paved and lighted path across the campground toward my fifth-wheel trailer, in much the same way an exasperated nanny would haul a temper-tantrum-throwing toddler out of the supermarket.

I tripped and hurried to keep up. Her pace didn't allow for objections or complaints. In fact, I was wheezing from lack of oxygen, she walked so fast.

Under the last maple tree before my campsite, she halted, still gripping my arm. "Pete's here, and he's not leaving until you talk to him."

"Oh, no." I swung around to retreat.

"Oh, yes." She jerked me back. Leaf shadows cast by a lamppost dappled over her face, giving her an eerily fierce look. "It's clear the two of you are madly in love, but you're being a ninny about it."

"Me?" I squeaked.

"Yes, you." Mom cupped my face in her hands and leaned in. Her eyes were dark and huge in the gloom. "I saw how you looked at him at church—wide open." She paused, and her gaze flicked away, then back again, boring into me with her eyes. "Wide open. Baby, don't let that go. For once I know what I'm talking about." She gave me a smack on my bottom and a shove toward the campsite. "Go."

CHAPTER 7

Pete was hunched in a lawn chair, elbows on knees, twirling the end of a stick in the dying embers of a campfire. He seemed to be concentrating, or mesmerized by the flames.

I stopped outside the campfire's glow, trying to figure out what to say—or what not to say, what to ask and what not to ask—and rubbed the stinging spot my mother's hand had left. Apparently, I haven't outgrown the application of physical discipline, at least in her mind.

Tuppence had followed me—ever faithful, ever present—and decided, at that moment, to shake. An ear-slapping, jowl-slinging, tag-jangling, full-body shake.

Pete stood quickly. "Meredith?"

My heart lurched at the worried look on his face. I knew in an instant—my mother was right.

I stepped into the light and closed the gap fast. Pete caught me and held me so tightly I couldn't breathe.

"I'm sorry. I'm sorry. I'm sorry," I whispered into his chest.

"Babe." His ragged breathing ruffled my hair. "You were just—gone."

I shuddered a deep breath, and Pete shifted, bending his cheek against mine, his day's growth of beard scratchy—and so real. I closed my eyes—I needed him real.

"I'm sorry," I whispered again.

Pete tipped my chin up. "This is my fault. I need to explain." He ran his thumb along my jawline. "Will you listen?"

I nodded.

He led me over to the picnic table. I climbed up, sitting on the top with my feet on the bench, facing the river. A giant, apricot-colored moon was nearly clear of the eastern horizon, its craters like dusty bruises in the fruit's flesh. I felt as though I had its full attention as it tipped over the highest range of hills—black bumps in the distance.

Pete scooted in snug beside me. "I'm keeping you close enough to grab in case you decide to vanish again."

"I'm sorry."

Pete cradled me, tipping my head against his shoulder. "I know you've been hurt in the past and had good reason to leave then, but this is not one of those times. You want to know about Tiffany?"

"Not really." I sniffed. "Um, yes—okay."

"High school. We dated off and on for a couple years. I knew it would never amount to anything, but it was fun—and she wasn't a cheerleader. Back then, I drew the line at cheerleaders."

I pulled back and scowled at him.

Pete's face dropped. "You weren't a cheerleader, were you?"

I snorted in the negative. I can't even clap on the two and four beats during a song, so twirling and flipping in synchronized rhythm was out of the question. Not that I wasn't a teensy bit envious of the cute girls who could do all that and keep perky smiles on their faces.

Pete squeezed me. "I'm sure there are smart, classy cheerleaders somewhere, but there weren't any in Platts Landing when I was in high school, and, anyway, all the football players wanted to date them. Guess I bucked the trends, even then."

"Football players would have outnumbered cheerleaders, what—four, five, to one?" I asked.

"Well, there was that, too." A smile played at the corner of his mouth.

"Was Tiffany the valedictorian?"

"Not hardly. President of the drama club." Pete ran a hand over the stubble on his chin. "It appears that hasn't changed."

The harvest moon was sliding up the side of a tree trunk, heading for the leafy canopy. A solitary cricket tuned his wings.

"So Tiffany grew up here?"

"Yep. On a farm out on Zimmer Road. I heard her folks sold the place a few years ago."

"Did she look, um—the same—in high school?"

Pete grunted, a sort of choked chuckle. "No. It took me several minutes to recognize her. I think she's had some, uh—surgeries. And grown a few inches maybe."

"It's the shoes."

"What?"

"Never mind. When was the last time you saw her?"

"Graduation—at the reception afterward she told me she was heading to Los Angeles for a screen test. I was scheduled to enlist in the navy a few days later, so we wished each other luck."

"Wasn't that hard?"

"Naw. We were interested in really different things. I got a few postcards from her, but her life seemed frenetic, disjointed. I didn't want that."

"Steady and sure," I murmured.

"What?"

"Mmm." I smiled up at him. "I like you."

Pete pulled me sideways onto his lap and nuzzled my neck. "Am I forgiven?"

"For what? My mother said I'm a ninny, and she's right. I'll try not to jump to conclusions in the future."

"Your mother," Pete muttered, "is something else."

"So it's not just my imagination?"

Pete chuckled. "But now I know where you get your spunk from."

"What do you mean?" I straightened and stared at him. "What did she do?"

"Set Tiffany straight about appropriate methods of greeting in three seconds flat."

I gasped. "What did she say?"

Pete opened his mouth, then closed it, then opened it. He exhaled. "I'm not sure—nothing overt. But there was definitely an undercurrent. Maybe it was just her tone. Tiffany backed off immediately and treated me as though I had a communicable disease the whole time I was helping Melvin set up their coach. By the end, it was like they were best friends—Tiffany was showing your mom her makeup kit for 'on-scene touch-ups,' she called it." Pete shook his head. "I don't know, but it was effective. I'm grateful."

"My mother, the fixer." I nestled back against Pete.

How does the moon move so fast? It was brilliant now, above the thickest lateral slice of atmosphere, and casting bluish-white light over the sparkling river. Our lonely cricket continued strumming, just in case a girl out there somewhere could hear him.

"I have to leave early tomorrow," Pete murmured.

I didn't move, kept my ear pressed to the regular thump-thump of his heart, hoping he could dally just a bit longer.

"Will you be here when I get back?"

"Always," I whispered.

Pete shifted me around so he could see my face. "Yeah?" His voice was hopeful.

I slid my arms around his neck and kissed him softly. "Yeah."

After Pete left, I climbed the steps to the trailer and opened the door. My mother and Tuppence had made themselves scarce. I stuck my head inside and listened in the dark.

"Mom?" I whispered.

The couch creaked, and Mom made gakky sounds, then started snoring.

I frowned and pulled the door closed behind me. My mother might admit to breathing heavily when she has a head cold, but she never, ever snores. Besides, she couldn't possibly have slept through Pete's firing up the motorcycle and leaving. No matter how quiet he was trying to be, Harleys just make a whole lot of racket.

My stomach growled audibly. I slapped a hand over my belly and glanced at the blanketed lump on the couch illuminated by moonlight streaming in through the window. The evenness and regularity of the nasal vibrations from that quarter sounded forced to me.

I grinned, wondering how long Mom could keep it up. I grabbed a packet of saltines and the peanut-butter jar out of the cupboard, then rattled the silverware drawer as I rummaged for a knife.

Still the feigned, evenly paced snoring.

I went up the steps to my bedroom, and just before I slid the pocket door closed behind me, I said in a low voice, "You were right."

I pressed my ear to the door. The snoring had stopped.

Tuppence roused herself from a catnap long enough to share in my midnight snack. Then she licked her chops, yawned her doggy peanut-butter breath on me, and went back to bed. Her snoring was not fake.

CHAPTER 8

How can two people live in such tight proximity and manage not to talk about anything personally important? I have no idea how this pattern developed, but my mother and I have perfected the dysfunction. The whole Tiffany-Pete-hiding-snoring episode went unmentioned in the morning. Mom didn't even ask if Pete and I had reconciled, but that might have been because my happiness was plastered all over my face.

Mom must have slept better, though, because she looked well rested and refreshed. The overhanging worry nagged itself back into my consciousness—the missing painting. I needed to pin Rupert down and get the complete history of Cosmo Hagg's artistic endeavors.

We'd just climbed into my pickup, loaded with insulated mugs of coffee and lasagna leftovers for a long day, when my phone rang.

I pawed through my purse. "Hello?"

"Ms. Morehouse? Leland Smiley here."

"Oh—Mr. Smiley." I scrabbled for a spare slip of paper and a writing instrument. Mom must have sensed my urgency and whipped a tiny notebook with a floral cover and a Cross pen from her purse. I smiled my thanks. "Since it's Labor Day, I didn't expect—"

"As an expatriate Brit, I keep to my home country's traditional holidays. Besides, how could I not delight in my work on such a glorious day? You appear to have an emergency."

"I do. I'd appreciate your help, but know you must have a backlog."

"Paintings that have already been stolen always take priority over those that are resting comfortably with their rightful owners—or in my workshop."

I breathed a sigh of relief. "So you'll perform optical microscopy on the paint chips?"

"Certainly, and whatever else may be needed. Send me as much as you can—the intact canvas strips would be best. And, my dear, use a courier service since your postal service is shut down today."

"Um—we're not exactly in a city that offers immediate service. The best I can do is UPS Next Day tomorrow for Wednesday delivery. What's your shipping address?"

"But where are you?" Mr. Smiley sounded shocked.

I explained our remote location.

"Ah, that is unfortunate. I do, however, have a trusted associate in Portland. I'm sure he wouldn't mind a drive in the country. I'll ask him to fly down to Los Angeles with your parcel this evening."

My jaw dropped. "Are you sure? It's a three- or four-hour drive, round-trip—and a plane flight." My brain was rapidly cha-chinging up the cost of such a venture.

"He'd like nothing better—you'll see when you meet him. And I actually prefer this method. I'm sure you can understand that the security of my workshop, with all these beautiful paintings in various stages of undress and stacked against the walls awaiting evaluation, is my utmost priority. The fewer delivery drivers coming and going, the better."

I exhaled. "I'll have everything ready when he arrives."

"Excellent. Now, my dear, I've studied the image you sent of the painting, and I'm terribly sorry, but I must ask—"

I cringed at the hesitation in his voice. "Yes?"

"The artist in this case—"

"Yes?"

"Was he of ill repute?"

I bit back a snort of laughter. "Not that I'm aware of."

"Shenanigans?"

"He's been dead for forty years, so I really couldn't say, but I don't expect anything out of the ordinary." I wrinkled my nose. "Um, but I'll pursue that line of inquiry today."

"I would, if I were you. Let me know what you unearth. It may help speed my analysis."

"Can I ask why you suspect—"

"Not yet. Just a hunch. But I will also keep you informed of the test results."

"But—uh—do you mean criminal?" I blurted.

"It doesn't hurt to ask, my dear. Now I really must go."

"Yes. Thank you. Good-bye." I hung up and scowled at the phone in my hand.

"Problem?" Mom asked.

"Maybe. Everyone who sees the painting seems to think Cosmo was either off his rocker or up to something."

A smile—wide and playful—spread across Mom's face, and her eyes sparkled. "Let's find out. This is so much fun."

I grinned back. "Now you know why I love my job."

ooo

The first task was prying Cosmo's painting's stretchers out of the frame. Mom and I dumped our stuff in my office, and I led her down the hall to the empty, looming frame, which still hung next to its descriptive plaque.

Mom stood, arms akimbo, and peered at the blank wall through the frame for a minute. She arched her brows and turned to me. "It has to be heavy. Do you have a step stool?"

"In the basement."

"Never mind." She stepped over to a marble-topped side table— one of the original pieces from when the mansion functioned as the Hagg family's vacation home. "This looks sturdy enough." She threw her weight against the far side and succeeded in budging the table a few inches.

"Wait a minute." I ducked to eye level with the table top and squinted. We don't keep the Imogene sparkly clean. It's impossible, for one, with all the cracks and gaps inherent in a century-plus-old building and the ever-present gorge winds, but it's also impracticable on our budget. Our exhibits are already old—a little dust isn't going to hurt them. Well, except the most fragile items, which I'd had encased in hermetically sealed display cabinets during the first year of my tenure as curator.

The protective layer of dust on the table top had been disturbed, and not by the cleaning crew. Mom joined me in a squatting position. One corner of the table had been wiped free of dust, but smudges— scuff marks?—were left in the dust's place. And in the center of the table a neat set of footprints were recorded, almost as perfect as those in the Chinese Theatre's forecourt. Semicircular sweeps in the dust ringed the footprints.

"Our thief had the same idea," I said.

Mom was scratching at a scuff mark with her fingernail. She lifted some black gummy residue. "Rubber soled."

"Half the shoes in Sockeye County."

Mom pursed her lips. "But not black tie. That would be leather-heeled for the men, and I don't see the small imprints of a woman's high heels."

"Actually," I sighed, "it's entirely possible someone wore sneakers with their tux or hidden by their long skirt. I didn't notice, but"—I shrugged—"around here, we wear what we have, and improper foot-wear isn't going to keep someone from enjoying a special event. We don't perform dress inspections at the door."

"But not necessarily from the night of the fundraiser, then?" Mom said it like a question, but she was right.

I hated that I hadn't noticed when the painting went missing. Why wasn't I paying more attention? I stood. "I don't know if this will be useful"—I waved at the tabletop—"since there aren't clear tread marks, and the dust may have shifted . . ." Enormously long odds. I sighed again. "I'll get the step stool."

Mom supported the frame from the bottom while I released the top from the wire hanging hooks. We eased it to the floor, facedown.

The back side of the painting, or what was left of it, was like a skeleton stripped of skin and flesh and all the elements that gave it vitality. Brittle canvas scraps clung to the edges of the stretchers like mummy wrappings, ready to disintegrate at my touch.

I levered a small crowbar around the edges and pried the stretchers—loose jointed but intact—from the frame. Half an hour sitting cross-legged on the floor with a heavy-duty staple remover completed the task. Mom collected the canvas scraps and the all-important paint tracings embedded in them into a manila envelope.

Footsteps sounded on the stairs, and Frankie's immovable brown helmet of hair appeared around the corner.

Her smile faded when she saw what we were doing. "Oh dear. It's not been found? I'd hoped, over the weekend, that—" Her brown eyes drifted over my mother, who was sealing the envelope.

I shook my head. "Not yet. I'm expecting a courier this afternoon, to pick up these fragments. This is my mother, Pamela Stephenson. Mom, this is Frankie Cortland, gift shop manager and event planner extraordinaire." I smiled at Frankie. I wasn't going to let Mom negate how wonderful Frankie had been for the museum—for me—with her pouting about not being asked to help. Mom could insert herself into the museum's activities if she wanted to, but only with Frankie's permission.

Mom rose and shook Frankie's hand. "So pleased to meet you." At least her smile looked genuine.

But my attention was diverted to Frankie's feet. From my spot on the floor, I had a good view of her sensible loafers.

"What size shoe do you wear?" I asked.

"Oh, um"—Frankie peered down self-consciously—"five, five-and-a-half sometimes. I'm short." There was a nervous tinge to her giggle.

And I realized what I'd done, drawing attention to Frankie's body while she was standing next to my slender, elegant, just-swooped-in-from-out-of-town, sophisticated mother. I jumped up.

"I was wondering because"—I pointed to the marks on the tabletop—"these appear to be of similar size. If that's the case, it would narrow the field considerably. Would you mind? Could I borrow one of your loafers for a minute?"

"Of course." Frankie slipped a shoe off and handed it to me, a worry crease between her eyebrows.

I held her shoe over the right footprint on the tabletop.

Mom leaned over, her head near mine. We were both eyeballing the difference in size.

"A quarter inch. Maybe half an inch longer," Mom breathed.

"What does it mean?" Frankie squeaked, trying to peek between us.

"Whoever stole the painting isn't much taller than you," I said. "He pushed this table over and stood on it to cut out the painting. Well, that's the current hypothesis."

Frankie's eyes widened. "I could go through the list of guests and mark the short people. Most of them I know, but if I don't, I'll ask around about their heights."

"Perfect. Now we're getting somewhere." I darted to my office and returned with a digital camera. I bent for the best angle to show off the dust and quickly snapped a few shots of Frankie's loafer on top of the footprint with the gap in sizes fairly evident. "I don't know if Dale can use this, but it's worth documenting."

"Halloo," Rupert called up the stairs. He was glistening by the time he arrived, and pulled a handkerchief out of his back pocket to wipe his brow. "It's a pity you can't take the day off. We're a dull set, laboring on Labor Day."

"Nonsense," Frankie chirped. "We get the best visitor counts on national holidays." She slipped her loafer back on and gave me a slight nod, which meant she'd ferret out the short people on the fundraiser guest list with the same single-mindedness Tuppence exhibits when she's flushing rabbits. I grinned as Frankie scurried down the stairs.

Rupert stuffed the handkerchief back in his pocket and captured Mom's hand. "And you are?"

"Pamela Stephenson, Meredith's mother."

"Ah, yes." Rupert cast a glance at me. "I see it, in the—in the— well, in the demeanor, and the bone structure, and the—well, about the face." He squinted at me. "Hmm. Your father must have been a remarkable, handsome man, Meredith."

I gaped. I think my mother might have a few grainy photos of my father, but he's a faint, faceless memory for me. I don't know where the photos are, but I would love to have them—if she doesn't want them anymore. But that was another thing I could never discuss with her. Since when did Rupert become an expert on human breeding that he could tell by looking at me? Or was he commenting on Mom's taste in men?

I caught sight of Mom's face out of the corner of my eye. She was gaping, too, and the fingers of her free hand were trembling.

"Rupert," I blurted, "I really need to speak with you about Cosmo, his history, anything you remember. Leland Smiley was asking."

"Leland?" Rupert released Mom's hand. "I haven't seen the old bloke in ages. He's doing the microscopy? He is the best . . ." Rupert's words trailed into a mumble as he pivoted toward the stairs. "Come with me," he called over his shoulder. "We'll dig through the files."

Mom clutched my arm and spoke in a hoarse whisper. "I'll wait in your office."

"Then call Alex," I muttered. "He's worried about you." Might as well toss all the cards on the table now. "I quit running last night. It's your turn."

CHAPTER 9

One of my ongoing—and it will probably take forever—projects is digitizing the Imogene's records. Whenever I have a few spare minutes, I scan in a handful of the miscellaneous documents that tend to accompany and provide provenance for works of art. As I sort through what's in the basement, I've been adding as much as I can.

But the only database Rupert uses is his own brain and a wall full of four-drawer filing cabinets in his office. When Rupert said we'd dig through the files, what he really meant is first we'd spelunk through his clutter, then we'd try to figure out his filing system, then maybe we'd start sorting through files. Mentally, I rearranged my calendar for the rest of the week to allow for the time this process would take.

Technically, Rupert would qualify as a hoarder. The problem is the haphazard mounds that have swallowed his office furniture include everything from letters to Meriwether Lewis signed by Thomas Jefferson, to the crust of yesterday's tuna sandwich. I can't just order a dumpster parked beneath his second-floor windows and start tossing his junk overboard because too much of it is of historical or artistic value. Most of what's in his office is his personal collection, but he's also the inheritor and—until I came along—keeper of the Imogene's records.

The best thing I could do was try to prod Rupert's memory while we were bushwhacking a trail toward the filing cabinets.

"Was Cosmo your uncle?" I called as I stacked a couple of boxes.

"No." Rupert's voice was muffled by the object he was wrestling— was it a cowhide? His upper half was hidden by something hairy and floppy. He was struggling to tuck its irregular edges into a neat roll.

"What is that?" I asked.

"Commemorative calfskin from the 1911 Pendleton Roundup. Cosmo was my dad's cousin, somewhat removed, not sure how far."

"Literally or figuratively removed?"

"Both. He was from the California branch, but the family moved here soon after he was born. Raised here, but lit out for the big city— New York first, then Los Angeles, if I remember correctly—as soon as he could. This is not firsthand knowledge, mind you, but Cosmo was the source of many back-of-the-hand stories in my family. Adults regularly rolled their eyes and commented on his troubles in terms us kids weren't supposed to understand."

"He ever come back to visit?" I shifted a pile of yellowed newspapers onto a packing crate.

"Whenever he needed money. Hence the eye-rolling."

"Did he get what he wanted?" I quickly flipped through the newspapers. The Paris Peace Accords dominated the headlines.

"Probably. He was a smooth talker. Always up to some scheme or other."

"But he had plenty of funds if he could donate so much along with the painting; $85,000 was a lot forty years ago—it's a lot now."

"Maybe one of his rackets paid out." Rupert grunted as he rolled a smooth, oblong piece of driftwood the shape of a giant pickle out of the way. He balanced a bulging expandable file folder on top of the chunk of wood and brushed his hands together as if it were a great accomplishment.

I wrinkled my nose but refrained from asking what Rupert's plans for the log had been. Instead, I ducked back to my task—a shoe box that had split and spilled its postcard collection. "Cosmo doesn't seem like the philanthropic type."

"Nope," Rupert huffed. "I do remember Dad's astonishment at the donation. But Cosmo had borrowed enough money from the family over the years; maybe he considered it a form of repayment."

"Did you—or your father—get the impression Cosmo was wrapping up loose ends with the donation?"

"Couldn't tell you. I was away at college then. I knew the museum would be my responsibility one day, but you know"—Rupert stopped to grin around the unlit Swisher Sweets cherry cigar he'd clamped between his teeth as fortitude against our monumental task—"I might have had other things on my mind at the time. If I remember correctly, her name was Ruby." He frowned and scratched his ear. "Or was that Celeste?"

I bent quickly and rummaged in a crate of papier-mâché dragon masks to hide my surprise—Chinese New Year, probably early 1960s. I'd thought Rupert was contentedly, if absentmindedly, single. Apparently not in his youth. I smiled to myself. That slice of his life certainly bore more investigating. I'd been worrying about him anyway—he wasn't in the best health, and at his age—fifty-nine—and with his travel schedule, he could stand some company. Maybe I could do a little matchmaking on the side.

I didn't have a large roster to select from, though. Sockeye County is rather lacking in single women of a certain age—or of any age, for that matter.

Cosmo—right. I was here because of Cosmo. "He died shortly after the donation, right?"

Rupert grunted assent. "A few months, a year or so, later. Freak accident—a sneaker wave off the Columbia River Bar."

The Columbia River Bar is one of the most treacherous stretches of navigable water in the world. There's a reason the US Coast Guard runs its Advanced Helicopter Rescue School out of Astoria.

"He'd taken a couple of his cronies out for a chartered fishing trip," Rupert continued. "His body washed up three days later."

"Were the rest of the passengers and crew ever found?"

Rupert glanced at me quizzically. "Sure. They returned to port. Badly shaken, but there wasn't anything they could do."

"You mean—?" I frowned. Cosmo's obituary had been seriously lacking in what I considered pertinent details.

"Cosmo was the only one washed overboard. He'd taken off his life jacket because he felt he couldn't manage his pole properly with it on."

I shoved aside a plastic Alpenrose Dairy crate containing books so old they were held together with rubber bands. "Where'd the Hagg family money come from?"

Rupert snorted. "Well, it's not illustrious, if that's what you're wondering. Cosmo was an outlier regarding risky business ventures, but not by much. In the early days of commercial transportation on the Columbia, there were a few upstanding capitalists who held virtual monopolies on the movement of people and goods, and even the production of those goods. My ancestors had shares in several companies, and their activities included things like colluding with Chinese mob bosses to man the fruit and salmon canneries, undercutting competitors until they went bankrupt, and stripping the forests."

Rupert straightened to wipe his brow with the handkerchief. "I think that history is what prompted turning this old place into a museum. The most recent couple generations of Haggs have wanted to make reparation for the family's past pilfering—a way to return some of their shadily gotten gains to the community." He sighed. "Not that there's much left anymore."

I nodded. The Hagg Family Trust made adequate provisions for adding to the museum's collections, but the founding board members had forgotten the old mansion would need tending to as well.

We'd planned the fundraiser in order to be able to perform basic maintenance on the Imogene. She was quietly and elegantly cracking to pieces under our feet. We desperately needed an outside infusion of cash to hold her together for the next generation. The Imogene has my complete devotion—we'll keep her running, even if she does appear to list to port.

"Sheriff Marge wants to know if we'll offer a reward for information leading to the safe return of Cosmo's painting," I said.

"I don't see the point," Rupert grunted. "But I suppose we could spare a few thousand out of the acquisitions allowance. I'll leave it to your discretion."

Rupert and I made good progress and reached the bank of filing cabinets just after lunch. I could tell Rupert was fading, and he mentioned needing to pack for his upcoming trip to Ireland.

"Do you mind if I carry on without you?" I asked.

"No, please." He waved dismissively. "You'll make more sense of the files than I could." He patted my shoulder. "What would I ever do without you?"

"Get buried alive in here?"

Rupert chuckled. "Probably. Keep me updated with Leland's results."

"Send me something nice from Limerick."

"I do have a couple appointments with local antiques dealers and an ironmonger."

"Let me know if I need to build a display for ancient hinges and locks. That would be fun." Asking for advance notice regarding Rupert's purchases is a futile plea, but I try every time.

"Of course, my dear." Rupert shuffled toward the door.

"And take care of yourself," I called.

He waggled a finger in the air in acknowledgment before he disappeared around the corner.

ooo

I poked my head into my office, hoping to relieve my mother of the boredom of a morning by herself. She had settled at my desk, my encyclopedia of Victorian majolica spread open before her.

"How's Alex?" I asked.

Mom's head jerked up, and she nearly tore the page she was about to turn. "You startled me."

"Alex?"

Mom flinched and swiveled the chair toward the window, blinking rapidly. "Not now, Meredith. Not yet."

"How long is he going to wait?"

"I don't know," she whispered.

I sidled around the desk and knelt in front of her. "Why won't you tell me?"

Mom traced a finger along my cheek. "Do you want to know how imperfect I am?"

"Frankly, yes. That would help a lot," I blurted.

Mom's tears were falling freely now. "I'm scared. This time it's beyond my control."

"Isn't it always? The idea that we humans are in charge of anything is a delusion, don't you think?"

Mom sniffed. "Pretending makes us feel worthy."

"Therein lies the problem. Would you like to talk to Pastor Mort? He's a good counselor."

Mom squeezed my shoulder. "Maybe—later."

Her jaw was set, and she was swiftly wiping the tears away. The gap in her veneer had just snapped shut.

I sighed and stood. "I have the world's worst filing system to sort through, and I could use some help. You game?"

Her eyes lightened for a brief moment. "Sure."

Mom caught her breath when I led her along the narrow swath Rupert and I had cut through his life's history of collecting, but she didn't comment. I stopped in front of the row of filing cabinets.

"We're looking for anything relating to Cosmo Hagg—his family ties to the museum, donations—any mention, really. I'm especially interested if he ran in artists' circles—if he could have had access to paintings by famous or up-and-coming artists or hung out with serious art collectors in the 1930s to 1970s. I don't know if any of that would be in here." I swept a hand toward the cabinets. "What does a British forensic art examiner mean by the word *shenanigans*?"

Mom managed a pinched smile and tipped her head. "I'll start at this end."

Unfortunately, the files seemed to be organized by type of article donated—not by date or name of donor. I happened upon paintings pretty quickly and found a few more scraps relating to Cosmo's donation of his own work. His painting was filed under "other" as the medium—kind of hard to categorize fishing line and clumps of decoupage on top of acrylic.

One of the notes included the title he'd given the scene—*Salmon Cache*. Why didn't we know this before? I would have put the title on the plaque next to the painting. Not that knowing the title enhanced the viewer's appreciation of the composition.

Mom was moving through the files faster than I was—probably because she wasn't bogged down by the history of irrelevant items. I could spend years sorting through things like this, absorbing and assimilating the complete provenance of the Imogene's treasures. Once I've handled, organized, and arranged the exhibit of a collection, they feel like friends to me, and I become engrossed in their story.

"Meredith." Mom held out a yellowed paper. "Look at this."

I pushed a stack of manila folders off my lap and stood.

Mom handed me the list handwritten on ruled legal paper. "It looks like code, but Cosmo's name is here."

I glanced over the sheet. "It's a photo list. These alphanumeric tags are the way they used to designate duplicate copies of negatives." There were about a dozen entries on the page, and at the bottom a date—February 27, 1973.

"How long do you think it took Cosmo to paint the still life?" I turned back to the paper slips I'd set aside earlier.

"Depends," Mom said. "I'd guess a couple months at least if it's as thick as it looks. Those paint globs would need drying time to keep the design from becoming smeared or muddy."

I found the note I was looking for. "This says the painting was donated on November 2, 1973. Mention is made of the ornate frame, too, so Cosmo donated the work once it was completely finished, dry and framed—roughly eight months after those photos."

"This doesn't say he donated the photos. It's more like he's a subject in the photos. See these other names—Sam 'Juice' Junkerman and Charles 'Gnocchi' Nervetti. It sounds like they're group shots."

I chuckled. "What's with the nicknames?"

"We are dealing with a man named Cosmo," Mom pointed out.

A phone rang, a muffled buzzing from the direction of Rupert's submerged desk.

"I guess they liked to eat—and drink." I waded toward the noise. I plunged an arm into the tottering stacks of papers on Rupert's desk, rooted around, and pulled out the receiver. "Hello?"

"There you are." Frankie sounded breathless. "I tried your office, the basement, then remembered you were going to do research in Rupert's office. Are you okay?"

I laughed. "I may need a compass to find my way out."

"Well, hurry. The courier is here."

CHAPTER 10

I slogged my way to the door, dashed upstairs to my office to get the envelope containing the canvas strips, then clattered downstairs. By the time I reached the ballroom, I was gasping for air.

I suppose the man waiting at the gift shop entrance was of average height, but he was so broad and muscle-bound that his proportions were off, making him seem short. His clothing appeared to be painted on, the garments stretched taut over a form that would delight Michelangelo. He was bald, but the dark shadow on his scalp indicated he had intentionally shaved off a full head of hair.

Then he turned, and all I could stare at—rather rudely—was his perfectly waxed handlebar mustache. The ends twitched when he spoke. "Ms. Morehouse?"

"Yes. Um, yes." I shook his meaty hand, trying to place the accent.

"Right pleased to meet you. Maurice Banks." He sounded as though he was rolling ball bearings around in his mouth as he talked. The *r*'s slid into vowel territory. And then it hit me—Australian.

"That for me?" Maurice indicated the envelope clutched in my other hand.

I thrust the envelope forward. "I can't tell you how much I appreciate this."

"Always looking for a reason to go for a spin," Maurice replied.

I tipped my head and glanced out the Imogene's double glass front doors. A glistening, fire-red vision shimmered at the curb—all scoops and swoops and sexy curves, low-slung with wide tires.

"What is that?" My mouth hung open most unattractively. I may have been drooling.

Maurice grinned, the mustache curling up against his pink cheeks. "My LaFerrari. She's a beaut, eh?"

Of course the machine was a she. I nodded dumbly.

Maurice checked his watch. "I could spare a few minutes. Not too many cops around here, eh?" He winked. "Want to see her?"

Again with the nodding. My vocal cords had been rendered inoperable.

Maurice held the museum door open for me, and we moved out to the sun-drenched sidewalk. All the while, he waxed poetic on the glory of driving along the gorge in a fine car—tunnels, hills, blind curves through forests, then clear sky, open road, and flying beside the river. His eyes sparkled with enthusiasm.

Then Maurice turned his attention to the car itself and mentioned the 800 horsepower from the V-12 combustion engine and the 163 horsepower from the electric engine. A hybrid sports car—it seemed a quintessentially Pacific Northwest accessory for the discerning driving enthusiast. I bet Ferrari's copywriter had fun composing the advertising text.

Maurice popped open the door to show me the cockpit. His accent plowing through the list of numbers and features jumbled in my head. I wasn't getting as much meaning from the litany as he would have liked, but he clearly relished the details.

My thoughts were of a more practical bent. "You fit in here?" I pointed to the narrow, semi-reclining, black leather bucket seat. These cars should come with shoehorns.

"Where there's a will, there's a way." Maurice cast a sideways glance at me. "You'd fit fine, sweetheart. Shall I come again sometime and take you for a ride?"

I stepped back, flustered. "Oh, uh—I mean, of course—I'd love a ride. But I know you're in a hurry. Wait—" My mouth hung open for the second time in our short acquaintance as a few things came together in my mind. I held up a finger. "Wait. Do Ferrari and Lamborghini owners fraternize?" I asked.

Maurice's eyes narrowed. "So my competition drives a Lamborghini?"

"No, no." I waved a hand, trying to get Maurice to switch tracks. "It's just that our sheriff is in the hospital because of a Lamborghini." I explained about Sheriff Marge's unsuccessful pursuit and how the state patrol had tracked the car, too, but had been unable to identify the owner.

Maurice stroked his mustache while I spoke, absentmindedly perfecting its spiral. He nodded when I finished. "It's not uncommon. When someone finally springs for an elite car, they're often so strapped financially that they can't—or don't want to—pay the extra costs of registration and insurance. Plus, he might be avoiding registering the car here in Washington because then he'd have to pay sales tax."

"That'd be a chunk of change," I murmured.

"Rich people can be real tightwads. There are two groups that drive true sports cars—those who are trying to impress others, and those who love the experience, the performance, and don't care who is—or isn't—looking."

"It's the same with those who own art." I nodded.

Maurice grinned. "Which is how a couple of odd fellows like Leland Smiley and I can be friends. We tolerate each other's crazy passions." Maurice rubbed the back of his neck. "He's also my mother's cousin by marriage and pulls in a few favors from time to time. Not that I mind."

I chuckled. "So unregistered yellow Lamborghini owners—know any?"

"Nope. I only associate with the up-and-ups." Maurice winked. "But it's a small community and somebody will know somebody who knows. I'll find out what's what, sweetheart. You can count on it."

ooo

Mom and I moved from Rupert's office to the photo archive room, where the filing system is by subject matter first, then by date. Trying to find pictures of three guys doing who knows what took the rest of the day. Turns out the list Mom found wasn't of negatives, but rather of slides.

I recognized Cosmo right away. The images appeared to be of a backyard summer party. Croquet mallets, paper plates mounded with food, and lawn chairs featured as props, along with a soaked and bedraggled Irish setter standing in a kiddie pool in the background.

Except only the same three men were in each picture, either alone or in groups of two or three. In a couple of the slides, someone's shoulder, leg, hand, or a blur that could have been a running child appeared, but otherwise there were no indicators about the size of the party or who else was in attendance. I got the impression these photos had been selected from a larger original collection based on their subject matter.

My stomach growled as I dropped the slides into a polypropylene archive box and banded the lid shut. "Let's call it a day. The museum closed an hour ago, and I can examine these slides at home."

Mom pushed her bangs off her brow and sighed. The dark circles under her eyes had returned. I felt a twinge of guilt for working her so hard. She's probably not accustomed to being on her feet most of the day. She looked as grimy and sweaty as I felt. Rummaging through the Imogene's detritus brings one into contact with enough dust and cobwebs to rival a catacomb.

"Sorry I don't have a bathtub for a nice soak, but you can have dibs on the shower while I pull together some dinner." I linked my arm through hers and guided her out to my truck.

OOO

Tuppence kept me company in the kitchen while Mom showered. I bent to scratch behind her ears and to scratch the constellation of mosquito bites on my legs at the same time—they were driving me crazy. My reward for falling asleep on the jetty yesterday afternoon.

Which made me think of Pete. I'm crazy about him, too, but in a completely different way. I grinned and dialed his number.

"Babe. What's up?"

"Nothing. How are you?" I wiped a dirty forearm across my forehead, pinned the phone between my ear and shoulder, and peered into the refrigerator.

"I keep thinking about what you said last night," Pete answered in a low voice.

"Mmm." I smiled, picturing him at the tug's helm, navigating the Columbia in the fading light, heading into the sunset. Someday I want to go on a job with him, just to spend time watching him in his world. I pulled out eggs, sour cream, blue cheese, and a red pepper. "How's the wheat?"

"Behaving itself. Any more interaction with your new neighbors?"

"Nope. But there are even more of them now. A mini city of coaches with California plates moved in today. I guess Melvin is serious about this documentary. No one was around when Mom and I got back from the museum, so they must be out scouting or filming somewhere."

I flicked on a gas burner, and the shower turned off.

"I only have a few minutes," I said. "Mom's about to join me."

"You holding up?"

"I guess. Not loving the ambiguity of the situation. She still won't talk to me."

"Sounds familiar." But I could hear the smile in his voice.

"Hey. I'm already disturbed by my similarity to my mother. I don't really need you pointing it out." I dumped scrambled eggs into a frying pan and moved to the sink.

Pete chuckled. "Patience, persistence, and a fair bit of cuddling."

"Huh?"

"It's worked with you so far. You might try it on your mom, except maybe not the cuddling part."

I plunked the washed pepper on the counter, flinging droplets everywhere. "I'm not sure how I'm supposed to take that. You mean you had this—me—planned out?"

"Of course. Ever since the football game you gave me a ride to last fall. Take it the right way, babe."

I scowled and slit the pepper, parsing it into tiny pieces—mincing it, actually.

Mom appeared at my elbow swathed in a robe, her hair damp. She nudged me out of the way and took over knife duties.

"Um, okay," I said into the phone. I wasn't sure what I thought about being the object of a strategic campaign on his part. But he was right about the effectiveness of his patience-and-persistence technique. And therefore, he might also be right about my mother. After all, where had I learned my reluctance to fully trust, seen it demonstrated my entire life? "I'll give it a shot."

"Call me tomorrow—a lot."

"I'm not the clingy type."

"No kidding. I just like hearing your voice and knowing you aren't stuck in a cave or being shot at. All right?"

"I'm not—" I started and then remembered that I'd been involved in things of that nature in the past. "Okay," I whispered, and hung up.

"You're looking a little ragged around the edges, just like your museum." Mom scraped the pepper pieces onto the eggs and lifted the edges of the omelet with a spatula. "Is there a salon around here? My treat."

I stared at her back, clenching my teeth. Patience and persistence—yeah, right.

"I was letting my hair grow for the fundraiser, so I could have an updo. But, yes, I need a trim now," I gritted out.

"Your nails? How about a facial?" Mom sprinkled blue cheese on the omelet, portioned it neatly in half, and slid it onto two plates.

"Today was like every other day at the museum for me. I'm not in the public eye most of the time. No need to impress anyone." I dropped into a chair at the dining table.

Mom plopped dollops of sour cream on our omelet and slid a plate in front of me. "Well, I could use some pampering. A mother-daughter day out. What do you say?" Her hazel eyes were worried, hesitant, as she sat across from me.

Is that what she really wanted? We'd just had a mother-daughter day. Granted, we'd been slaving away in a dank, old museum. I sighed. "I'll call Barbara at the Golden Shears tomorrow. See what she has open."

OOO

After dinner, Mom insisted on cleaning up. I could tell she was exhausted, but she wasn't going to kick me out of my own living room so she could go to bed. And I was restless. If I stuck around in that confined space with her much longer, I was going to say something I'd regret later.

Tuppence poked my shin with her cold nose, giving me just the excuse I needed. If I could get her really tuckered out, maybe she'd snore less tonight.

"I'm taking the dog out," I said. "It's been a few days since she's had a good run. You don't need to wait up."

Mom wiped her hands on a dish towel and nodded, the same worry lines still creasing her forehead.

I wanted to suggest again that she call Alex, but figured nagging had lost its effectiveness a while ago. Even Alex had told me she needed time. But how much? I let the door slam behind me.

Tuppence shook, jingling her tags, and set off directly for the path that circled the campground, her nose running zigzag patterns an inch above the grass. I swung into my long-strided hiking gait in order to keep pace with her, feeling the good stretch in my calves and thighs.

I inhaled deeply, savoring all the scents that come with this time of year—tangy, sweet fruit rotting under the trees, harvest dust drifting down the gorge from the big wheat farms upriver, lazy water—the lingering, brackish hint the river takes on in late summer when it's not moving as fast and the lower levels expose more mud on the banks.

Tuppence looked back to make sure I was following, snorted, then resumed her exploration, white tail tip serving as my guide. Two juvenile ospreys circled overhead, calling to each other with piercing cries. I chuckled. The young ones always sound a bit panicked, as though once aloft, they start nervously contemplating how to get back down.

My most effective antidote to stress is a ramble—preferably a ramble with a view. There's something about being in a place untouched, or at least unhindered, by humans that helps put irritations and frustrations into proper perspective.

At the end of the campground, Tuppence and I forged our own path along the riverbank, climbing over boulders and downed trees that had come to rest in the mud. We investigated gravel bars and backwater eddies, startled frogs and killdeer, were chattered at from the brush by chipmunks and a baby raccoon that was out early and apparently without parental guidance.

Tuppence wanted to bring the baby home with us, but after much cajoling on my part, she reluctantly left it. As soon as she turned her back on the raccoon, it let out a rattly practice hiss of false bravado. I laughed. But give it another couple months and it would be a full-grown creature to be reckoned with.

Darting black forms caught my eye—swallows? No—bats skittering over the water, starting their nightly feeding. I glanced around. It was later than I'd realized. The tips of the small chop on the river twinkled in the last of the sunlight.

I snapped my fingers for Tuppence and turned. Within a few minutes, we were moving more by feel than by sight. I grumbled under my breath as I clawed my way over a hip-high rock, scraping my knee on its rough surface. This was a great way to get a twisted ankle. Why hadn't I been paying attention?

Tuppence, with her four legs, is much more sure-footed than I am. She scrabbled ahead, returned to check on me, then darted out to the lead again, thus covering three times the distance I did—good for sleeping later on, but a little annoying at the moment.

"Yeah, yeah," I muttered the fourth time Tuppence panted on me. "I'm coming." I bent, hands on knees, to catch my breath. Surely I was taking the longest, hardest route, but I couldn't see well enough to find the easy way.

The campground's lampposts came into view, blinking between tree trunks and silhouetting the row of California motor coaches.

"You're dead," a male voice growled.

I froze, my heart pounding into overdrive.

A furry body brushed my legs—Tuppence back on a welfare check. I grabbed her collar, feeling for her tags and clenching them in my fist to keep them silent. I crouched beside her.

Was he talking to me? How could he even see me? I fought to keep my rapid breathing quiet, even though the sound of it was rushing through my head.

I glanced down at what I could see of my clothes in the dark, trying to remember—yes, a blue chambray blouse and khaki skirt. And white legs. I had a summer tan, but on me that doesn't mean much. My legs glowed like bleached sticks. I yanked my skirt hem down over my knees and tried to get lower.

Then I realized there was another voice—whiny but too low-pitched to be feminine—another man.

"Quit mumbling or I'll rip your tongue out," the first voice said. His consonant stops slid slightly, as though he had a speech impediment or his dentures weren't quite lined up. He had the vigorous voice of a healthy man, though.

I had to agree with him. I also wanted to hear what the second guy was saying. I strained forward.

"I need time—time to e-s-s-stablish a connection one cannot go barging in without credentials and s-s-some expertise—"

My eyes widened. Melvin Sharpe. Melvin of the run-on sentences. Even though anxiety—or fear?—had raised his voice an octave, I recognized it.

"If that broad distracts you, I'll take her out first."

My breath caught in my throat. Did he mean Tiffany? Who else around here would qualify as a broad? Of course, to some men all women are broads.

"S-s-s-source she knows where to find it we'll start tomorrow rest as-s-s-ured you'll—" Melvin whimpered.

"Shut up. You get on my nerves. You're also on borrowed time." Brush crackled and heavy footsteps thumped first on dirt, then on the paved path.

I ducked, then immediately popped up, craning my neck when I realized the man was walking away from me.

But nothing—all darkness, not even a flicker of movement to indicate his size or height.

Then Melvin sniffed—loud and very close.

I dropped to my knees. I didn't want him to know I'd witnessed yet another impingement on his manhood—first Tiffany, now this unknown goon.

Melvin slunk by, clearing his sinuses with wheezes and hacks. Allergies or was he crying? Good grief.

A minute later, a door on Melvin's coach clicked open and closed just as softly. I scooted up to the paved path and tiptoed past the film crew's campsites, then raced for my trailer, Tuppence on my heels.

Was the other man a member of the crew? Melvin hadn't seemed surprised, just defensive. I would be, too, given what the goon had said. Death threats? But I was irritated that Melvin hadn't fought back. He was making himself an easy target.

As I locked the door and crept through the dark kitchen to my bedroom, I listed my own problems—a recalcitrant, sofa-surfing mother, who was sleeping soundlessly tonight, a stolen painting, and a good friend in the hospital with a broken leg. I wasn't sure I had the mental space to worry on Melvin's behalf, too.

CHAPTER 11

I showered quickly, bending in half in the skinny stall to examine my bruised, scraped, and bug-bitten legs. I'd need to wear pants tomorrow or people would wonder what I'd been up to.

I considered calling Sheriff Marge or one of her deputies about the overheard threats. But Melvin was as capable of dialing 911 as the rest of us if he wanted to, and I didn't think law enforcement could do much about hearsay on my part without him initiating a request for help or protection.

Still damp and appreciating the sensation of cool cleanness after a day of sweaty scavenging, I flopped on the mattress and pulled the shade off the bedside lamp. I popped open the small box I'd brought home from the museum and removed the slides of Cosmo and his friends.

I held them in front of the bare bulb one at a time, squinting to see if I could pick out any telling details. I was willing to bet the stubby blond guy with the prominent belly was the one nicknamed Gnocchi.

That left the tall, gangly one as Juice. He didn't look like much of a drinker—not much flab on him, nor redness about the nose. The tips of his face—nose, chin, ears—stuck out, giving him a unique silhouette, and his arms, legs, and fingers seemed disproportionately long. I wondered if he had the same disorder people used to think Abe Lincoln had—Marfan syndrome.

Juice was dressed in a snug leisure suit with an abundance of pleated patch pockets and flared pant legs—the cutting edge of fashion at the time and probably custom-made to fit his narrow height. Beside him, Cosmo and Gnocchi looked downright frumpy in baggy suits with neckties loosened and collars unbuttoned.

Three overdressed guys at a barbecue—they stuck out as loners among what were probably family activities going on around them. It just seemed weird. Weird in general—what were they doing at the party? And weird, specifically—why were these images part of the Imogene's photo archives? What had Cosmo been up to, besides eating baked beans?

ooo

When we arrived at the museum the next morning, I set up Mom with a sorting task—a box of impossibly jumbled Bakelite earrings I'd found in the basement. At the rate I was unearthing costume jewelry down there, we'd soon have a display of zany things women have adorned themselves with over the centuries. This particular box held earrings replicating foods and flowers.

I felt guilty about it, but I also felt as though I needed to stash Mom somewhere for a while—for her own safety, and mine. I'm so accustomed to doing my own work, going about my own business, and having the freedom to adjust my schedule accordingly, that having a dependent in the form of my mother was wearing my patience thin, and I was frustrated by my lack of productivity.

I snuck up to the library/taxidermy exhibit and called Dale. I wished I'd been able to pop in and visit Sheriff Marge since her discharge from the hospital, and I was anxious for word on her health as well as her frame of mind.

"She's in the office for the first time today," Dale said in a hoarse whisper. "Hang on."

I heard a door slam and heavy, thudding footsteps and knew Dale had just exited the modular building that served as the sheriff's department command center and was now out in the weed-infested parking lot, probably leaning on his cruiser.

"I don't know how we're going to manage this," he groaned. "She's just not accustomed to being confined to a chair, or to a cast, for that matter."

"How about a casserole?" I asked.

"Noooo," Dale almost shouted. "We're up to our eyeballs in casseroles and Jell-O salads and rolls and cobblers and pies and—shoot. Why do people assume you need to eat more if you're injured?"

I chuckled. "We're sorry we can't make her feel better, so we're hoping to distract her, and all of you, with full stomachs."

"What she really needs is a problem to solve—one that doesn't involve interrogating witnesses on scene, wrestling bad guys to the ground, or high-speed chases. And I think Hallie could use a break at home, too."

I bit my lip. I should have thought of relieving Hallie sooner. "No word on the painting, then?"

"Nope. That's just it. The doldrums. Usually summer's busy—lost hikers, drunk boaters, farm accidents, grass fires—one thing after another. We're having a real lull. We don't even have anybody in jail right now, so all us deputies are sitting around, and Sheriff Marge is stewing up a storm."

"There's a film crew staying at the Riverview RV Ranch—" I started.

"They being disorderly?" Hopefulness tinged Dale's voice.

"Threatening, maybe. I overheard something last night. Along the lines of do-it-or-you're-dead."

"We haven't had any reports or complaints. Who were the parties?"

"That's what I thought." I sighed. "Melvin Sharpe was on the receiving end. I didn't recognize the other guy."

"Sharpe? He's the director, right? I think I met him at the Imogene fundraiser. Tall, scrawny, glasses. Couldn't tell a calf from a colt?"

I snorted. "That's him."

"He jumped a mile when Zach fired his shotgun during the demonstration. I was standing next to him and practically had to catch him on the way back down. Bundle of nerves, that guy."

"Or just a city dude."

"Huh." Dale's grunt indicated exactly what he thought of a man so out of his element. "The fellas and I'll take turns driving through the campground the next few days while they're here. Make sure they realize we're paying attention. Maybe that'll put a lid on any hanky-panky."

"And if it helps, the Imogene can offer a small reward—say, up to $5,000—for info leading to the recovery of the painting. Maybe that'll speed things up for you." I cringed at the number, but anything less wouldn't be motivating.

"Gotcha. We've had zilch, but if something comes up, we'll let you know."

I hung up and heaved a sigh.

"You okay?" Frankie called from the doorway. "I heard talking and was pretty sure it wasn't the animals, but you never know."

I patted the snarling cougar's head and strode toward Frankie. "Dale was just complaining about not having enough to do, and I was thinking I have too many things to worry about—too many unknowns."

Frankie chewed on the end of the pencil she held between two fingers, making me wonder if she was a former smoker. "No word on the painting, then?"

I shook my head. We were starting to sound like anxious twins.

"Oh dear. Well, I do have some good news." Frankie bounced on the balls of her feet and pursed her lips.

I tried to peer at the notebook in her other hand, but she pulled it away.

"Wait—" She beamed. "We spent $7,237 on food, catering staff, decorations, signage, invitations, and demonstration supplies."

"Whoa." My mind jumped to the red numbers that probably just appeared at the bottom of our annual operating budget.

"After expenses, we netted $38,231 from the fundraiser."

I clamped a hand over my mouth, my eyes bulging.

"I know!" Frankie squealed. "Can you believe it?"

"You're amazing." I grabbed her in a big bear hug, and we did a jig in the doorway.

"Did I miss something?"

I tried not to groan and turned to face Mom. Frankie shrank like a scolded child.

"I had a question about categorizing these." Mom held up a couple of pairs of earrings—purple grape clusters and lemon drops.

Frankie stuffed a paper into my hand, whispering, "Here you go, honey." She darted a nervous glance at Mom, then said, louder, "I'd better get back to the gift shop." She scurried down the hall in the opposite direction.

I checked my watch and clenched my jaw. The museum, including the gift shop, didn't open for another half hour. My mother emits an aura that makes people—my friends—give her a wide berth. This was nothing new—I'd grown up with it. But I hadn't asked her to come here, to create social discomfort in my carefully orchestrated realm.

I had no idea why Mom had taken a liking to Pete—enough of a liking, anyway—to insist I reconcile with him. I was glad she had, but still—

I closed my eyes. I was going crazy.

"Meredith? These are part of necklace-and-bracelet sets. Do you want the sets kept together or separated by piece?"

"Sets together," I gritted out. "I'll come help you clear space for arranging the items. We'll need to take documentation photographs."

"What did I interrupt?" Mom whispered as we clumped down the basement stairs.

"The fundraiser cleared almost $40,000."

"Meredith, that's wonderful." Mom's eyes were bright. "This community must really value the museum—and appreciate you." She squeezed my arm.

Was that how my mother measured approval? I sighed. "We had a lot of out-of-town guests. I suspect that's where most of the money came from. Sockeye County's not exactly booming." At least she was pleased—for the moment.

Mom had made good progress on the jewelry. I quickly became distracted examining the juicy fruit, the brilliant flowers, and a few creepily realistic insects she'd spread out on the top shelf of a padded transit cart. I reached to snap on a spotlight and remembered Frankie's paper.

I uncrinkled the page and squinted to decipher Frankie's loopy handwriting.

"What's that?" Mom leaned close.

Frankie had underlined the title of her list—Short Fundraiser Guests. She'd organized the list by height, from 4'10" to 5'3"—bless her heart—with each name followed by an estimate of the person's stature. She'd even included her own name, toward the top of the list.

I joggled in silent laughter while skimming my finger down the page. If these poor people only knew we were now analyzing them by linear inch instead of for their potential donation capacity. The vast majority of the names were women's.

"Do you know any of them?" Mom asked.

"Most, but I wouldn't suspect a single one." My finger hovered over Barbara Segreti's name. "This reminds me—I need to call Barbara for appointments for you and me this afternoon."

"She runs a spa?" Mom asked hopefully.

"Not exactly, but it'll do. You'll see." I drummed my fingers on the transit cart and grinned. "I have another idea. You good for a few minutes?"

Mom nodded.

I zipped upstairs and, from the privacy of my office, dialed the newest grandmother in Sockeye County.

"Yeah," Sheriff Marge grunted.

"How are you feeling?"

"Not worth mentioning. Your mom still with you?"

How does she home in on the main issue so fast? "Yeah. I have a couple favors to ask, one of which might not be exactly appropriate."

"Yeah?" I could hear the arched eyebrow in Sheriff Marge's tone.

I took a deep breath. "First, are you up for babysitting the adorable Jesamie this afternoon and maybe into the evening?"

"Course I am," Sheriff Marge huffed. "I'm not an invalid."

"I just wanted to make sure, with the cast and all—"

"I haven't forgotten the basics. Since she isn't crawling yet, we spend most of our time snuggling and looking at books anyway. She doesn't cry when she's with me."

I smiled at the pride in Sheriff Marge's voice and the idea of her peering through her reading glasses, doing the voices for classic children's stories, and pointing to the pictures. She could pull it off. I'd love to sit on the floor and invisibly listen in.

"Then Mom and I would like to kidnap Hallie around four o'clock—maybe it could be a surprise?—and take her to the Golden Shears for a little pampering. Sound good?"

"Exactly what she needs. Perfect. Ben's going nuts without her, and I feel bad she's been cooped up with me. She's sweet, but"—Sheriff Marge heaved a sigh—"I guess I'm accustomed to my widow ways. I like things to be where I left them."

I chuckled. "You and me both. Which leads to my second request." I lowered my voice and pushed the door closed. "Mom."

"What about her?"

"She's hiding something. Won't tell me. I wonder—I guess it's possible—if maybe she's divorcing my stepfather. He doesn't seem angry, but he is worried about her."

"He's contacted you?"

"Once. Told me to give her time and take care of her."

"Huh. She done anything like this before?"

"Not that I know of. But my family's not exactly forthcoming. Is there a way you can check, without doing anything illegal, if she's been arrested or named in a police report? I don't know—I hate to think it, but maybe drugs? Or a DUI? Shoplifting?" I dug my thumbnail into the edge of the desk. "I'm grasping at straws here, but what would embarrass her so much that she won't tell me?"

"Uh-huh," Sheriff Marge muttered. Soft scratching rustled in the background—she was taking notes.

I was spying on my own mother, but I'd just given Sheriff Marge a problem to solve.

"You have any joint accounts with her?"

"Bank accounts?" I asked in surprise. "Not since I turned sixteen. Why?"

"You know her financial situation?"

I frowned. "No. I can't even watch her spending habits here, because what is there to buy? I could ask Alex, but that would arouse his suspicions if he doesn't already have them. I don't want to add fodder if a divorce is in the works."

"I'll see what I can do." Sheriff Marge clicked off.

I slipped into the hallway and dragged the frame from Cosmo's painting into my office. I'd left it tipped against the wall below its attribution plaque yesterday in my hurry to question Rupert and dig through his files.

Now, the big empty spot gnawed at my imagination. What had Cosmo's intentions been? From his pictures he didn't seem like the type of man to enjoy painting as a hobby, and even more certainly not the type to inflict his artistic expression on others. He'd looked like a harried businessman. Then again, Winston Churchill had dabbled in painting, and he also wasn't the type you'd think would do so based on his appearance.

The last thing I wanted to do was advertise the painting's absence. I stood the frame on its short side and wedged it behind the door. I grabbed a screwdriver from the bottom drawer of the filing cabinet and removed the plaque from the hallway wall.

I shoved the marble-topped side table over, rummaged a ghastly and gigantic dried-flower display from the Victorian ball gown exhibit, and plunked that on the table. It sort of masked the screw holes and smudge marks from the hanging wires—my best solution until we could get the wall repainted. If people didn't know what they were looking for, they might not notice.

CHAPTER 12

Mom and I established an efficient rhythm and emptied enough boxes of Bakelite that I needed to assign identification numbers so I wouldn't confuse the pieces. Mom manned the digital camera, while I checked in each image and arranged the basic documentation information in folders on my laptop.

The lights in our improvised photo studio create a lot of heat, and I was starting to wilt when a "Yoo-hoo!" came from the stairs.

I blinked toward the dark end of the basement, and two forms—one tall and lanky, and one curvy and blonde—appeared.

"Frankie said you'd be down here. Isn't she a sweetheart?" Tiffany gushed.

I groaned inwardly at the sight of them, but I'd promised my assistance when I met Melvin at the fundraiser.

"Ooooo, Bakelite." Tiffany snatched up a cherry charm bracelet and slipped it on her wrist.

"Don't touch," Mom snapped. "These are official museum pieces."

Tiffany hastily pulled off the bracelet and dropped it back on the transit cart. "Sorry." She retreated a couple steps and clung to Melvin's arm.

Melvin cleared his throat.

I wondered if Mom knew something I didn't about Tiffany's habits. Maybe she'd gathered a few hints the other day during their bonding session in the motor coach.

Melvin cleared his throat again, and I decided to take pity on him. "How can I help?" I asked.

"Oh, just perusing the museum for old times' sake Tiffany's that is from her school days seeing what she remembers and—" He shrugged and pursed his lips. The action raised his glasses on his ears, making him look uncannily like an academic, beatnik weasel. Like a malignant creature from *The Wind in the Willows*.

I took a deep breath. I had to stop my personal dislike of these two from interfering with professional courtesy. "I'm afraid we don't have any exhibits relating to food. Well, other than this jewelry"—I jabbed a finger at the transit carts—"or locavore culture. We should. It would certainly be appropriate, but it's an area the museum's lacking in."

"What about salmon?" Tiffany asked. "I remember this really huge, horrible painting that had a fish on it and used to hang in the ballroom. We always started with that painting when we had school tours even though everyone hated looking at it."

A stab of surprised worry made me inhale too fast, too obviously— but I tried to recover and appear nonchalant. "I'm sure you've noticed a lot has changed at the Imogene since you were in grade school. We try to rotate through exhibits to keep things fresh." Which wasn't exactly true, but was technically true in the case of Cosmo's *Salmon Cache*. I guess you could say the painting was out on involuntary loan. I just didn't know who to. And I really, really hoped its "loaning" wasn't going to have negative repercussions for Rupert.

"Have you been to Willow Oaks yet?" I continued. "I'd be happy to call the owner, Dennis Durante, and introduce you if you'd like. He's produced several award-winning wines from his vineyard, and he has a farm-fresh menu at the attached bistro. It would be a lovely, scenic spot for filming."

Melvin dipped and bobbed and acknowledged he'd appreciate my making the connection for him. I trotted upstairs to use the phone in the gift shop.

Dennis became so excited he was stuttering by the end of our conversation. They say the camera adds ten pounds. I hoped, for Dennis's sake, that it could also add ten thousand more acres of grapes; a larger, sundrenched patio; and maybe some insulation in the pole barn that housed the bistro. His property does have an amazing view of the Columbia, which I hoped Melvin would be able to capture to advantage.

What Dennis really needs is a business manager so that he can focus his energy on what he does best—tinkering with flavors. You never know, though—Dennis and Melvin seemed cut from the same habitually nervous, high-strung, artistic cloth. Maybe they'd hit it off.

I also took advantage of the softly creaking quietness of the big mansion's main floor to place another promised call to Pete. He didn't answer, which is not unusual given his demanding job, so I left him a cheery, I'm-surviving-with-only-my-sanity-intact message.

When I returned to the basement with a quickly scribbled map and directions to Willow Oaks, I pulled up short of the group, suddenly struck by a sense of unease. Tiffany and Mom were chatting while Melvin stood silently by, still trying to figure out what to do with his hands and feet. But the women's amicability was all on the surface. Mom was practically bristling with distaste, her mouth curled in a little sneer—a look I know well. And it was clear that Tiffany had interpreted the look correctly. She was struggling to keep up a light conversation, her tones wary.

I now knew that whatever friendship Pete had thought he'd witnessed between these two Sunday night was his wishful thinking—or an incorrect perception based on the fact that he doesn't know my mother very well yet. And if Tiffany's spent the past decade or more in Hollywood, she's probably very different from the person he remembers, too. Women have an amazing capacity to spread a smooth fondant layer over the nastiest hardtack below.

I glanced between the two women in the strong shadows cast by the spotlights. Add a couple six-shooters and Stetsons and we'd have an old-fashioned gunfight on a Burbank back lot.

"Well, then," I said brightly, stepping forward, "Dennis is thrilled. He's expecting you." I handed the map to Melvin.

"Thanks so much," Tiffany called over her shoulder while ushering Melvin out of the basement.

"Well," Mom huffed.

"Why do you dislike her?" I asked.

Mom turned to me, wide-eyed. "You're one to ask."

"You mean because of Pete?"

"Pete's not the problem. He's all yours—in case you hadn't noticed." Mom glared at me, then jerked her thumb in a very unladylike manner toward the stairs. "She's the problem. That glossy, ditsy exterior is intentional and meant to hide the conniving schemer underneath. Maybe she has designs on Pete, but I think it might be something else. She's the type to use others to get what she wants. Melvin doesn't stand a chance."

"Maybe you should know—" I murmured.

"Know what?"

"I overheard someone—a man—threatening Melvin last night. And the threat included Tiffany, as though she might become collateral damage."

"A member of the crew?" Mom's brows shot up.

"I didn't see him. But I'd recognize his voice if I heard it again. A bit slurry. Heavy breather. If his body matches his voice, he's a big guy."

Banging rattled the basement door, and I nearly jumped out of my skin.

Mom slapped a hand on her chest. "What is that?"

"Phew." I shook my head. "Sabretaches." I jerked the door open in the middle of another round of banging.

"Hey, there," Derek, the DHL delivery guy, said from behind a stack of boxes. "Sorry I didn't have a chance to text you. But you're always here anyway. Where do you want 'em?"

I stepped back. "Anyplace you can find room."

Derek shimmied the stack off his hand truck and bustled up the ramp outside for another load.

"Sabretaches?" Mom asked.

"The precursor to the fanny pack. Go ahead and open it." I handed her a box knife. "Just be careful with the blade. I don't know how well they're packed."

Mom lifted a packet shrouded in acid-free paper from wads of bubble wrap. She carefully peeled back the layers. "Oooo."

Derek returned with the remaining boxes, then cast a glance at Mom, who was caressing the embroidered flap of a worn leather pouch. "Wish I could stay for all the excitement."

I signed his digital clipboard. "We'll put you to work."

"In that case, I gotta go." He cracked a grin and shut the door behind him.

"I wouldn't be caught dead in a fanny pack," Mom said. "But this would make an amazing handbag."

I slipped my fingers through the metal rings at each corner of the pouch and slung it at arm's length from my waist. "Originally, they were designed to hold fire-starting supplies and other necessities before pockets were common. Later on, they became dispatch cases for military officers and couriers, typically hung from the sword belt like this, and often having a rigid flap that doubled as a writing surface."

"A man purse." Mom giggled.

"Shows they like decoration as much as we girls do." I spread the other sabretaches from the top box on a cart. Their ornamentation ranged from regimental crests to silver embroidery in a dense, allover pattern. "They demonstrate the textile and leather-tooling techniques of the time as well."

"Beautiful," Mom breathed.

Bakelite or sabretaches? We were running out of space on the transit carts. You can see how difficult my job is. Since the jewelry was already partly documented and consisted of so many tiny, fiddly pieces, I reluctantly shoved the sabretache shipment to the side. Maybe I could get to them next week.

ooo

On the drive to Sheriff Marge's house, I filled Mom in on the surprise relief mission we were running for Hallie. Mom perked up at the idea of throwing a mini party for someone she'd never met.

True to her word, Sheriff Marge hadn't uttered a peep to Hallie, so it took a few minutes to convince her to, one—come with us, and two—leave Jesamie behind. But once safely squashed between Mom and me on my pickup's bench seat, the sparkle in Hallie's eyes told me she was going to enjoy the treat.

We left Sheriff Marge ensconced in a padded rocking chair on the front porch with her leg propped on a footstool and Jesamie on her lap, all necessary supplies for whiling away a few hours piled on a table beside her. As Sheriff Marge held Jesamie up and helped the baby wave bye-bye, I was struck by how disturbingly alike they looked. Add a few wrinkles to the pudgy cheeks, replace the bald head with tufted gray hair and a pair of reading glasses, and they could be cross-generational twins. They had the same serious steel-gray eyes and steadfast gaze that ensured you could never put anything past them, as well as the "Try me" scowl—intimidating on Sheriff Marge, disconcerting on Jesamie.

The Golden Shears isn't technically a beauty salon. It's a barber shop that Barbara inherited from her father. She cuts hair for humans—and animals—of both genders. I'd been startled, and a bit squeamish, the first time I had to wait for Barbara to finish blow-drying a poodle before I had a turn in the chair. But Platts Landing is far too small to support a dog groomer, and not many people around here fancy the high-maintenance breeds anyway. Barbara meets her clients' needs as best she can.

Her secret is a small back room with a couple of lounge chairs with foot basins and the girlier accoutrements of nail polish, wax, tweezers, body scrubs, and the like. I pushed open the shop's glass door, smiled to Barbara, who was wrist-deep in shampoo suds, and led Mom and Hallie straight through the beaded curtain to our hideout, which I'd booked for the rest of the afternoon.

"You two go first," I said. "I'm next in line for a haircut."

"Is it—self-service?" Mom glanced around the room.

"You just turn on the tap. Barbara will be in later for the polish phase."

Hallie grabbed a jar of Epsom salts and dumped a scoop in each basin. "I haven't done this since before I got pregnant." She scooted into a chair, slipped her shoes off, and dipped her feet in the warm water. "Heavenly."

Mom handed her a couple of gossip magazines and climbed into the other chair. She shot me an I-can't-believe-you-dragged-me-into-this-dump look. I shrugged. Then she leaned forward, squinting, glanced quickly at Hallie, who was already flipping through an old issue of *People*, and gestured for me to turn around.

The wall behind me was covered with framed photos—a kind of family history of the barbershop. I'd seen them before and had thought it odd that Barbara kept photos—mostly black and white and of men with close-cropped hair from the *Leave It to Beaver* era—in a room that was dedicated to the more feminine pleasures. I swiveled back toward Mom, palms up. What did she want?

She jabbed her finger lower and to the right and mouthed the word, "Cosmo."

I spun and stooped, scanning the pictures. Sure enough. Cosmo and his two buddies—Juice and Gnocchi. It was the same image as one of the slides. Had Barbara's father taken the picture? Was the barbecue held in the Segreti family's backyard?

"Meredith," Barbara called from the front room, "the chair's open."

Mom and I shared a look. Should I ask Barbara about the family connection? Mom pressed her lips together and scrunched her shoulders.

"Meredith?" Barbara called louder.

"Coming." I hurried into the barbering area and slipped into the elevated chair, still warm from the last occupant.

In the mirror, I caught the eye of a lavender-haired old lady who was regarding me with particular curiosity.

"You're that museum gal," she shouted over the roar of her dryer hood.

I nodded and smiled. I wouldn't be able to grill Barbara under these conditions.

"I want the recipe for the chili," the old lady shouted. "You know— from the fundraiser." She gripped her chair arms with frail, blue-veined hands and lurched forward as much as the hood would allow. "No gas afterward. Never had that before from chili." She shook her tightly permed head. "Must be a secret ingredient."

"Something's wrong with you, then, Hazel," shouted a henna redhead at the other end of the dryer-hood row. Her face and visible cleavage had more wrinkles than an elephant's hide, and she wagged a pink acrylic-tipped finger. "Could be your digestion's blocked up."

"How you doing, hon?" Barbara bustled over. "Trim? Your hair sure grows fast in the summer." She ran her fingers through my brown curls, then wrapped a plastic cape around my neck and prodded me toward the wash stations.

"I met your new temporary neighbor yesterday—Tiffany Reese. Knew her as a girl, too, but she sure has changed," Barbara said in a low voice, leaning close. "You know she and Pete—but that was ages ago. I never did think that pairing would last long. Pete's far too sensible, and he has you now." She nudged me with her elbow. "Brought her current boyfriend along."

"Melvin?" My mind was jumping around, trying to keep track of the undercurrents in Barbara's words.

"Mmm-hmm. Tiffany was wanting a few wholesale cosmetic supplies, said she really has to make some of the subjects up so they look decent for the camera. Said she considered me a mentor when she was in high school." Barbara snorted softly. "I barely saw that girl. Always buzzing about with her own ideas and never settling down for a real conversation, know what I mean? I didn't teach her a thing—certainly not how to look the way she does now."

I slouched in the chair and tipped my head back into the basin.

Barbara stretched over me to grab the shampoo bottle, dragging her polyester sleeve across my face. "Do you know anything about the boyfriend's family or where he comes from?"

"Melvin's? No. I haven't been that sociable with them."

"Oh, I understand, hon. Of course. But you needn't worry. Pete's so head over heels over you, there's no recovering. I can tell just by watching the two of you together. We're all waiting for him to pop the question." Barbara patted my shoulder.

I stared at the water-stained acoustic ceiling tiles while Barbara doused my head and decided—just for a few minutes—to forget about the gossip and the robbery and the threat against Melvin and my irritation with Mom and Cosmo's checkered past and Pete's former girlfriends.

Barbara's fingers worked magic on my scalp. Just for a few minutes I'd think of nothing at all.

CHAPTER 13

My relaxed state lasted through a pedicure and facial, through listening to Mom and Hallie chattering happily about not much on the return trip to Sheriff Marge's house, and through a simple dinner of—yet again—grilled cheese sandwiches.

Again, Mom insisted on cleaning up, so I stepped outside to replenish Tuppence's rations and share a sandwich crust I'd saved for her.

"Pssst!" Tiffany's head popped out of the shrubbery at the edge of my campsite, past Mom's parked Mercedes, just as I turned off the spigot.

Tuppence growled.

I dropped the full water bowl. It made several revolutions on the wet pavement before coming to a clattering stop against the trailer's wheel.

"Can I talk to you for a minute?" Tiffany waved me over.

"In the bushes?" I asked. Dumb question. But really—had she been stalking me?

"Quick. Before your mom sees us."

My mouth fell open.

Tiffany grabbed my arm and pulled me along the path to the river, moving amazingly fast for the pair of lemon-yellow, patent-leather, peep-toe platform pumps she had on. I stumbled and slid in my sandals, my heels still slick from the pedicure lotion.

"Come on," Tiffany hissed, giving my arm a yank.

"Just a minute." I jerked away from her grasp. "This is outrageous." I almost said, "*You* are outrageous," but I bit my lip instead.

"Please?" Tiffany's eyes welled.

I wondered just how much of her emotion was melodramatic acting. I crossed my arms over my chest and scowled.

Tiffany cast an anxious glance back at my trailer, then ducked around a thimbleberry bush. Before I could stop her, she squatted low in some upstart poison oak. She held a finger to her lips and motioned me to join her.

Normally, Herb Tinsley, the owner of the Riverview RV Ranch, wages successful war against poison oak. This little clump must have escaped his vigilant zeal. The reddish leaves—*leaves of three, let them be!*—were brushing against the backs of Tiffany's thighs, which were exposed even more than usual with her miniskirt hiked up from squatting. She should have recognized the plant, since she grew up in Platts Landing. Her time in Hollywood had made her rusty.

Half of me—okay, maybe more than half—wanted to engage Tiffany in a prolonged conversation, right there, without moving, but with my keeping a safe distance. I did need to consider my options for a moment.

Then I reached out and grabbed Tiffany's hand, hauling her to standing and clear of the poison oak. "You need to wash that off, right now."

"What? Where?" Tiffany hopped around trying to see her behind. "Get it off me!"

"Too late," I muttered. "You have calamine lotion?"

"What? Oh, no. No! No, no, no, no." Tiffany had spotted the poison oak and started peeling her skirt off.

"Wait," I hollered. "Let's go inside."

"I'm allergic. I'm so allergic," Tiffany moaned.

"We'll try superhot water. I've heard it intensifies the itching but also gets it over sooner." I escorted her to the motor coach and prepared the way for her so she didn't have to touch anything like door handles or faucets.

We huddled in the bathroom—no matter how glamorous an RV is, the bathroom is always minuscule—and I cranked on the shower to full hot. Steam enshrouded us as Tiffany disrobed.

"Toss your clothes in the bottom of the shower so they don't touch anything else," I ordered. "Stay under the water until you can't stand it." I rummaged through the medicine cabinet and found a lotion with aloe vera on the ingredient list. I plunked the bottle on the counter and slid the door closed behind me.

In the galley kitchen, I lathered to the elbows—twice—just in case I'd inadvertently come in contact with any of the urushiol from Tiffany's clothes. I soaked and squeezed two dish towels, then loaded them with ice cubes and folded them into thirds. I opened drawers until I found Ziploc bags to seal the ice packs.

The shower was still running. I had no idea where Melvin was, but he clearly wasn't present. What would you do? Yeah—me, too.

The token office/desk area in the motor coach was a mess. I uncovered a marked-up script and scanned it quickly. Whoever wrote it didn't know the first thing about locavore culture, or about writing clear descriptions, for that matter. I hoped Melvin and crew would interview Dennis to get their facts straight. I found a list of desired backgrounds and types of locations, and another list of foods the crew thought they could feature. Boy, these people really were from a concrete jungle—they had no concept of farming, climate zones, irrigation, or what could and could not be grown in the Columbia River Gorge. I returned everything to its slipshod place.

Then I flipped through a worn, expandable leather briefcase that sat open on the floor next to the desk—a few manila folders, AC adapter for a laptop, highlighters, a pair of sunglasses. I pulled out the folders, and my breath caught in my throat. The top folder was labeled "Imogene."

I opened the folder, and pages slid to the floor. As I scrambled to retrieve them, the shower turned off.

Someone—Melvin, or Tiffany?—had printed out the history and contact pages from the Imogene's website, public information. But what made my heart stop beating were the hand-drawn floor plans—all four floors. The rooms and passageways were marked with bold capital letters—ballroom, kitchen, Rupert's office, servants' stairwell. The drawings were rough and not to scale, but they were certainly sufficient to direct someone how to maneuver through the mansion.

They were also old—or at least the information regarding exhibit locations was old. A few rooms had notes about the exhibits on display, and they were incorrect. Under my direction, the taxidermy exhibit had been moved to the library to provide an environment that was better for the preservation of both the books and the animals. We'd also expanded the gift shop and moved the Native artifacts into more prominent locations. So the information on the floor plans predated my employment at the Imogene.

The bathroom door thumped open. "Meredith?" Tiffany called.

I jammed the folders back in the briefcase and jumped up. "Coming," I shouted. "Just stay there—you need to rest. I'll bring a compress."

Tiffany, wrapped loosely in a bath towel, was sprawled on her stomach on the California king bed—her skin bright red from the recent scalding. She struggled to dab lotion on the backs of her thighs.

"I can do that—if you don't mind." I perched on the edge of the mattress next to her.

"Would you?" Tiffany groaned. "I can't believe this happened to me."

She lay still as I gently applied lotion to the huge welts already rising. Then I balanced the ice packs on her legs.

"I think you're going to be either lying on your stomach or standing for the next few days. I'm sorry." And I meant it. Poison-oak rash would be an effective torture method.

"I wanted to ask for your help," Tiffany sniffled.

"There's nothing else I can do for you. I really am sorry. When the itching becomes intolerable again, get back in the shower. Alternate hot water then cold compresses. It'll be awful but maybe not last as long. If you start swelling anywhere else or have trouble breathing, you'll need to go to the hospital."

"No, I mean help for Melvin."

I slid onto the floor and sat cross-legged facing the bed so I was at Tiffany's eye level. The memory of the threatening goon's voice flashed through my brain. "What do you mean?"

"He's such an idiot." Tiffany managed to make the statement sound affectionate. She sighed. "I guess that's the curse of artistic genius. No common sense."

"You think Melvin's a genius?" My nose wrinkled, quite involuntarily.

"Oh, yes." Tiffany propped herself up on her elbow. "Brilliant. Did you know he only films on the old-style thirty-five-millimeter celluloid?"

"And how is that good? Not for longevity."

"It's all about expression, grittiness, obscure reality." Tiffany's eyes widened—the dazed groupie look.

I wondered if she knew what those words meant. She sounded as though she was reading from a brochure. "So why does he need help?"

Tiffany deflated. "Money."

"Making documentaries is expensive?"

Tiffany grabbed a pillow and wadded it under her chest. She rested her chin on her hands, her wet hair clinging to her shoulders. "Worse than that. He borrowed money to finish his last film. It was so great.

And he was so sure he was going to receive a Sundance production grant, but it fell through."

"Has the bank called the loan?"

Tiffany snorted. "No bank lends money for a film unless you're Martin Scorsese or somebody."

My stomach dropped—that explained the goon. "How much time does Melvin have?"

"Every week it doubles." Tiffany sniffed again and pressed her palms over her eyes. "What are we going to do? We have to keep carrying on like everything's normal, or the crew will desert us. But they're getting cranky because they haven't been paid in a while. We just need a little more time—time to finish this film. We'll enter it in all the festivals—it's bound to win something."

I grimaced inwardly. Based on the script I'd seen, the documentary would never make it into a juried competition, no matter how amazingly retro the cinematography was.

"What is it you think I can do for you?"

"Your boss—he's rich, isn't he? Could you put in a good word for us? We just need some funds to tide us over."

My eyes narrowed. She wanted to borrow money from Rupert? What were the museum floor plans for? This little scheme had the hallmarks of a shakedown. But I couldn't be sure they'd had anything to do with the painting theft. They'd just arrived in town the day of the fundraiser, and I couldn't imagine this pair pulling the theft off on such short notice. Besides, if they'd stolen the painting, why specifically ask about it this afternoon?

In icy tones, I informed Tiffany that Rupert was one, out of the country, and two, dirt-poor when it came to cash, since all the family funds were tied up in the trust for the museum. Granted, he might appear as though he was jet-setting, but any money we had was narrowly earmarked for museum acquisitions only. I didn't think Tiffany needed to know about the success of the fundraiser.

"What are we going to do?" Tiffany clutched my arm.

"I'd tell the sheriff if I were you. She might be able to offer you protection—in Sockeye County, anyway."

"Oh, no." Tiffany drew back. "They said—" She shook her head. "No—no—we can't." She bit her lip as more tears came.

"Well, that's your call." I rose and stared down at her. She really was scared. And the way the goon had referred to her as a distraction didn't bode well for her future. "Even if Melvin won't take action, you need to—for your own safety. It's not too late."

"He needs me," Tiffany whimpered. "I can't leave him. He can't function without me."

I didn't doubt it. "Is it worth risking your life over? Melvin's life, too?"

"He's going to win an award." Tiffany blinked red-rimmed eyes. "I know it."

"Don't pretend with me. We both know that's not going to happen."

"Get out," Tiffany hissed. She flung an arm out, pointing toward the door, as if I didn't know the way.

I stepped back. "The sheriff's a friend of mine. I can help connect you with her if you want. But it'll only work if you're willing to face reality."

"Get out!" Tiffany dug her nails into the edge of the mattress, the muscles in her forearms bulging as though she was about to spring off the bed.

"You know where to find me."

I fled to the freedom of the outdoors and fresh air and the absence of hysteria. You know where to find me? Why on earth had I said that? Now I'd be jumping at every branch crackle and pinecone dropping on the lawn. I fought back the irrational fear that Tiffany would sic the goon on me. I wasn't sure she even knew about him.

Anyway, everyone knows where I live. Not exactly a secret. I trudged back to my campsite and scratched Tuppence between the shoulders.

"How good of a guard dog are you?"

Tuppence shook, slapping her floppy ears over her head and under her chin.

"That's what I thought."

CHAPTER 14

The next morning, after sleeping—not well—on it, I decided to inform Mom of the troubles next door. I figured she had a right to know since I'd sort of gotten mixed up in the mess as well, thanks to Tiffany. And in staying with me, Mom might be in harm's way.

She took the news remarkably well—silently, in fact, but with the little divot between her brows that indicated she was worried.

"So," I said breezily, "it would probably be best if we stuck together. No midnight ramblings"—I grinned sheepishly since I'm the one most likely to wander off—"or staying home alone. Besides, I appreciate all your help at the museum."

Mom stared down at her hands clenched in her lap on the drive to the Imogene. When I pulled to a stop in my usual parking spot, she was spinning her wedding ring on her finger.

"Who did Melvin borrow from?" she asked.

"Tiffany didn't say, exactly. Someone who thought it necessary to send an enforcer along."

"Shylocking," Mom muttered.

I bit back a smile. Leave it to my mother to phrase Melvin's problem in Shakespearean terms. "A loan shark, yeah."

Mom sighed. "I've seen that—seen what it does to people—good people."

"Who asked the wrong person for help."

"Who didn't have anyone else to ask," Mom said sharply, with some heat.

I stared at her, but she refused to meet my eye, still fidgeting with her ring. My phone rang. I heaved a sigh and dug it out of my purse.

"Meredith, my dear, it's not too early, is it?"

"Not at all, Mr. Smiley. I'm glad to hear from you."

"Well, I have bad news—or rather, bad news from my point of view since I find even the hint of scandal rather exciting. I suppose it will be good news for you."

"No older underlayers, then?"

"Acrylic paints through and through, consistent with an early-1970s estimated date."

"Thanks for checking, and for the expedited treatment. I can't tell you how much I apprecia—"

"You've been investigating the artist's past?" Leland interrupted.

"Yes, but we haven't—"

"Was he a jeweler?"

"I haven't uncovered a legitimate occupation. He seems to have been a bit of a schemer."

"I found a tiny trace of gold, just a few flecks. I thought perhaps from an accidental brush against his workbench or something, if he painted in proximity to a metalworking studio."

"The frame is gilded. It could have rubbed off."

"Unlikely. I'd call it gold dust, embedded in the paint, not on the surface. It's not unheard of—to mix gold with paints—but not like this. It was a technique usually selected for the purpose of embellishment, not overall, and certainly not hidden in opaque acrylics."

"But it could have been accidental?"

"That's my best guess. Coincidental contact during the course of painting. By the way, what did you do to Maurice, my dear?"

"Uh," I frowned. "Nothing?"

"We usually have quite a good chat when he visits, but he spent the entire evening muttering about a yellow Lamborghini and calling his friends. Then he dashed out to meet a dealer for drinks." Leland sounded as though he was pouting.

"Oh, that is my fault. I asked if he could, through his connections, locate the owner of the car that caused a friend of mine to collide with a tree."

"Nasty business. I'm sorry to hear that. Give my regards to Rupert." Leland hung up.

"Another dead end?" Mom asked.

I nodded. "The elusive Cosmo—or rather, the inexplicable Cosmo." I pounded on the steering wheel. "Why? Why would someone steal it?"

"At least now you can have a clear conscience about not having it x-rayed."

"But that means it was taken for sentimental or revenge reasons if not for the intrinsic value of the painting."

"You're worried about Rupert." Mom laid a hand on my knee.

I nodded. "I think the key lies in the Hagg family history."

ooo

I hate dead ends. And I couldn't really blame it on Mom, but her fidgetiness had rubbed off on me. I'd exhausted the possibilities of finding out more about Cosmo in Rupert's files. My options were to continue puttering around with Bakelite and sabretaches or switch to doing something physically demanding to burn off my frustration. Or I could crash a party.

Near lunchtime, I suggested the idea to Mom. "Want to go see how the documentary is progressing at Willow Oaks? We could grab a couple sandwiches in the bistro—innocuous cover for a little reconnaissance?"

"Oooo." Mom perked up. "I've never been on a film set."

"Me neither." I grinned.

For the first time since I'd lived in Platts Landing, parking was scarce at Willow Oaks. Mostly because a couple of the California motor coaches were angled awkwardly in the gravel lot, without regard for anyone else who might want to approach the tasting room. I pulled onto the grass under an apricot tree.

The uniform for the film crew seemed to be monochromatic—black jeans, tight black T-shirts, black motorcycle boots for the men, and black strappy sandals for the women (which were not terribly practical on gravel). Black mascara, black eyeliner, and stark black brows for the women, too. Tiffany stood out like a gaudy Mardi Gras bauble in an emerald-green sundress with a very full skirt, her blonde hair piled high on her head. The dress was a good choice for hiding the aggressive, blistering rash I knew must be all over her backside by now. I wondered what kind of painkillers she was on.

I wasn't too anxious to bump into Tiffany, though, so I directed Mom around the far side of the pole barn and through the open kitchen door. Dennis's seasonal assistant, Saskia Worthington, had a sandwich assembly line going, her fingers flying across the crusty rolls, distributing a greens mix, halved cherry tomatoes, and cucumber slices.

"For the crew?" I asked.

Saskia wiped sweat from her nose with her forearm. "Yeah. Hope they're happy. Never met a pickier bunch. Vegans, gluten-intolerant, lactose-intolerant, onions-give-me-heartburn, and the 'I'll only eat it if it wasn't breathed on by migrant workers' subset." She rolled her eyes.

"Do you mind?" I pointed toward a cooler of bottled beverages.

Saskia waved permission.

I grabbed two sweet iced teas and handed one to Mom. "When you're finished feeding the crew, we'll take whatever's left over. No special requests."

Saskia laughed. "You should check out the filming. Poor Dennis. He's holding up okay, but that director . . ." She rolled her eyes again.

"Bad, huh?"

"We agreed to do the documentary because the publicity—any publicity—is good. Being so far from a metropolitan area, it's hard to entice visitors. But now I'm not so sure." She shook her head and slapped fresh mozzarella slices on half the sandwiches. "Poor Dennis."

I frowned and glanced at Mom. She shared a concerned look with me.

We slipped out to the patio and found a table in the shade with a good view of the action. The crew had rolled a few wine barrels out of the cellar bunker and propped them in front of the open sliding doors. They formed a backdrop for Dennis, who was perched on a stool. Two soft boxes on extension poles hung over him.

Melvin was like a jack-in-the-box, popping out from behind the camera to flap his disproportionately large hands while reviling the crew, swearing, shouting, or cueing Dennis. He pushed his glasses up to his forehead and blinked sweat out of his eyes before hunching down to the viewfinder again.

Dennis shifted on the stool, prompting an exasperated gesture from Melvin. He scooted back into position, shoulders hunched.

Tiffany descended like a brightly colored vulture and poked at Dennis's face with a makeup brush. Then she blotted his receding hairline.

I opened my iced tea and took a swig. I kept cringing at Dennis's unease and glancing away. He didn't need more witnesses to his misery. Watching a film session wasn't nearly as entertaining as I'd thought it would be. No one seemed to be having a good time.

"What?" a voice behind me barked. "Look, he's your liability."

Some of the tea went down the wrong way, and I sputtered. It was the voice—the goon. I didn't dare turn around.

Mom whacked me on the back.

A large man—clothed entirely in black just like every other crew member—came into my side view and tossed a backpack onto a chair at the next table. "You gotta make up your mind," he growled into the cell phone pressed to his ear. "You want me to shake—" He spun away and stalked out of sight around the back of the pole barn, presumably for privacy for his call.

I held up a hand so Mom would stop hitting me and tried to catch my breath. "He's the one," I rasped.

"Which one?" she whispered.

"The enforcer."

Mom's eyes narrowed and she glanced over her shoulder. "He's gone. We don't have much time." She shoved her chair back, the cast-iron legs screeching on the flagstones, and darted toward the man's backpack.

"What're you doing?" I hissed.

She already had the bag unzipped and was pawing through the contents. "Watch." She tipped her head in the direction the man had taken.

I half stood, still gripping the chair arms, and craned my neck, heart pounding, my eyes glued on the bushes at the corner of the pole barn. "Hurry. He's not someone to mess with," I said out of the side of my mouth.

"Oh, yeah?" Mom's voice was hard.

The man's conversation didn't last long, but we were lucky he had big feet. He kicked a flower pot on his way back around the corner.

"Now," I said through clenched teeth.

Mom rezipped the bag and scurried back to our table. She dropped into a chair, slipped a white envelope into her pocketbook, crossed her legs, and hiked her skirt a bit all in one smooth motion. She sighed audibly and glanced up at the man as he rejoined us on the patio.

She swung her top leg, her espadrille—yeah, that amazing espadrille—dangling from her polished toes, and flashed him a dazzling smile.

The man stopped midstride and stared at Mom. At least he didn't look at me—because I was still gulping air, guppy-cheeked. He nodded curtly. "Hello."

"You with the film crew?" Mom asked.

"Sorta." He ran a hand over his short hair, effectively revealing his ripped abs through his stretched T-shirt.

"Hmm." Mom took a sip from her tea bottle and returned her attention to the film set. She rested her left hand on the tabletop, and the diamond in her ring flashed in the dappled sunlight.

The man scowled, gave Mom one more thorough look-over, then slung his backpack over his shoulder and headed for the parking lot.

"Good grief, Mom. Didn't I just give you a cautionary lecture about this—this—" I ran out of words for the magnitude of our problems. "What are you doing?" My voice pitched up in irritation.

"Don't overreact." Mom removed the envelope from her pocketbook. "This looked like it might be interesting."

The envelope, crinkled and dirt-creased, was folded to size around the contents. Mom coaxed the envelope open and slid several photos out. She spread them on the table.

I jabbed a finger at the picture closest to me—a snapshot of Cosmo's painting, set on an easel.

Mom tipped up the photo. "This isn't the same image you have for museum documentation."

I shook my head. "Looks like it was taken before it was donated."

The other photos were eerily familiar—duplicates from the backyard barbecue featuring, again, Cosmo, Gnocchi, and Juice. How many people had had access to the negatives back in the day—or still? These guys seemed to have a regular paparazzi following.

Why was the goon walking around with a picture of Cosmo's painting? Was he looking for it, too? Join the club.

Faux Reel

I bit my lip as the thought sank in. If he *was* looking for it, and he was still hanging around, that meant he wasn't the thief. The same hypothesis ruled out Melvin and Tiffany as well—their unexpected interest in the painting during their visit to the museum yesterday indicated they didn't yet know it was missing. Or were they playacting?

Maybe I should be glad the painting had been stolen, if for no other reason than to keep it out of the hands of these three characters. But why would they want it?

"I don't know why I didn't notice before," Mom muttered. She was squinting at a photo she was holding at arm's length in front of her.

"What?"

She slid the photo sideways, then back again. "See the resemblance?"

"To what? You're going to have to help me out here."

"Melvin and this tall, dark man—Juice, was it?"

I darted a glance toward Melvin, in full director, arm-waving mode, then drew back to look at the skinny, stooped man standing next to Cosmo in the photo and holding a beer bottle in his overly large hand. Probably similar heights, certainly similar body builds, the same disproportionate limbs, but there are many tall, gangly men in this world.

Then Melvin turned, and I caught his pointy profile. "Oh!"

"See? Unmistakable."

"Thanks for waiting," Saskia called from the kitchen doorway.

Mom gathered the photos and dropped them facedown in her lap just as Saskia arrived with our sandwiches.

"He's kind of handsome, isn't he?" Saskia grinned.

"Who?" Mom asked.

"Vince. The big guy—muscles, military-cut black hair?" Saskia pulled a couple of napkins from her apron pocket and tucked them under our plates. "I saw him out here on the patio a few minutes ago. Doesn't say much, but he's been hanging around, kinda separate from the rest of the crew." She leaned over and whispered. "I think he's a bodyguard or something. He's carrying, concealed."

115

I almost dropped my dill pickle spear. "How do you know?"

"Saw a bulge at his waistband, in his center back, when he bent over once. I guess his T-shirt is too tight to hide a shoulder holster. But wouldn't an ankle holster be more comfortable?" Saskia shrugged. "Whatever floats his boat. Me—I prefer my bra holster. I have *three* girls." She winked and returned to the kitchen.

I scowled at my sandwich. I didn't know which was more disturbing—finding out that the goon was armed or that my food server knew so much about gun accessories.

CHAPTER 15

The afternoon seemed to drag on forever. Mom and I retreated to the coolness of the basement and exhibited remarkable diligence in documenting the Bakelite jewelry. But the task wasn't demanding, and left too many of my gray cells free to mull over my compounding problems.

I tried to separate, compartmentalize. I really had only one major issue—Cosmo's painting—where it was and what it was, or wasn't. So many question marks.

But other people's potential disasters swirled around, creeping closer and closer—Mom's secrets; Melvin's and Tiffany's financial woes; and the hired gun, Vince. The only thing I felt comfortable ruling out as cause for concern was Pete and Tiffany's past relationship. Tiffany was sticking with her man—Melvin. And that worried me even more.

A call from Maurice was the only highlight in the interminable hours.

"He's a sketchy fellow, but I found him," he said. "Yellow Lamborghini purchased through Freewald Luxury Motors in San Diego. He picked it up, straight off the freighter from Italy, at the Long Beach docks and drove it home. A whole string of sightings and chases by police in small coastal towns along Highway 101 about a month ago. The guy has a lead foot. On his own personal Cannonball Run or something."

"And you know his name?" I almost squealed.

"Better than that, sweetheart. I know his address, too. What did I tell ya about my contacts?"

"You're sure he's the one?"

"Only three yellow Lamborghinis have been purchased and delivered to the West Coast in the past eighteen months. The other two were properly registered by their owners in a timely manner, both in California. Nope, he's the only new yellow owner in the Pacific Northwest in recent memory."

"I owe you dinner."

"Dinner and a drive," Maurice countered.

"Deal."

Maurice rattled off the Lamborghini owner's information. I had him repeat it, with spellings, to make sure I didn't misinterpret his accented words.

After hanging up with Maurice, I checked the address online. The owner actually lived in Sockeye County, but just barely—out on barren rangeland in the northeast corner of the county, where he probably had room for his own private racetrack. Locally, the Lamborghini sightings had been only late at night or in the early-morning hours. Sometimes wealth exacerbates reclusive, antisocial tendencies.

I didn't want Sheriff Marge to know I'd been nosing about in her business, so I called Dale. "I have a bead on that unregistered Lamborghini."

I grinned at Dale's excited exclamation as he scrabbled for his notebook.

"How did you—? You know what—I don't want to know. What you got?"

"Friend of a friend of a friend. All legit and confirmed. I bet the closest neighbors could verify." I gave him the name and address.

"Shoot." Dale sounded immensely pleased. "I'll see if Judge Lumpkin would like to sign a search warrant."

"Gives you something to do, anyway," I said, still grinning. "You going to tell Sheriff Marge?"

"No way. She'd insist on going. Can you imagine? With that cast, hobbling around a ranch. I can't be responsible for her if she decided to accidentally smash the thing's headlights or add a few dents with her crutch. She's definitely carrying a grudge. Did you know this is the first time she's ever been laid up since she's been sheriff?"

"She's a trooper." I knew Dale was joking about Sheriff Marge seeking personal retribution. She's a stickler for the intent of the law. Sometimes she skirts around the letter of the law a little, if needed—the same way a mother would let a punishment slide if she thinks her child is repentant and has learned his lesson already. No point in heaping up consequences and damaging a person's reputation unnecessarily. "Just to check—no word on the painting?"

"Nope. Sorry."

"Okay." I sighed. "Have fun."

"You bet." Dale hung up.

ooo

Mom and I were following our evening ritual—the one we'd developed to have some alone time even though we were spending every day, all day, in each other's company. She was washing up the dinner dishes while I puttered around outside on the pretense of tending to Tuppence.

A white Ford Crown Vic with the county logo on the side pulled up in front of my trailer, and Dale climbed out of the driver's side. "Hey, Meredith." He hurried over. "I brought you a visitor." He glanced back at the car and said out of the side of his mouth, "She's determined to get out and about."

The passenger door slowly opened, and the rubber tip of a crutch hit the ground.

"Can I help?" I asked, starting forward.

"Naw." Dale grabbed my elbow. "She wants to do it herself. Besides, I need to tell you—" He turned away from the car to gaze at the river, still speaking. "Got the warrant. I figured you could keep her busy tonight while we—"

"What're you mumbling about?" Sheriff Marge's brusque voice sounded behind us.

"Just explaining the situation to Meredith, about taking you home later," Dale replied quickly.

"Sorry about that," Sheriff Marge huffed. "Until I get this thing off"—she smacked the side of her full-leg cast—"I can't"—she clenched her jaw—"drive." She peered at me over her reading glasses, and I realized how much she hated saying the word *can't*.

Mom pushed open the trailer door. "I thought I heard voices. Hello."

"Pam." Dale touched the brim of his Stratton hat to Mom, then he ducked his head close to my ear. "Okay?"

"Yes." I nodded emphatically so he'd know I meant yes to everything. I'd do my best to distract Sheriff Marge from wondering what her deputies were doing on such a fine evening.

We weren't off to a good start, though, because Sheriff Marge was glaring at us, back and forth between Dale and me.

"Right, then." Dale gave Mom one more nod and escaped to his car.

"How are you?" I started with a falsely upbeat smile.

"Gotta minute?" Sheriff Marge said in a low voice.

"Uh, yes?" I was planning on most of the night, but she didn't know that—I hoped she didn't, anyway.

"Privately." Sheriff Marge muttered and tipped her head toward the fifth-wheel.

I glanced up at Mom still in the doorway, and then it dawned on me.

"Mom," I called, "there's peppermint ice cream in the freezer. Could you load that between the chocolate cookies I made the other day? Sheriff Marge is staying for dessert."

Mom frowned, but her good breeding forced out a cheerful, "Of course." She disappeared into the trailer.

Sheriff Marge clumped over to the picnic table, managing her crutches surprisingly efficiently for not having much of a swinging radius, and eased onto a bench. "Got a visit at the office today from a repo man. I was alone when he came, so nobody else knows yet. That's why I had Dale bring me over, besides the fact I know I'm driving my deputies crazy. Thought it best to get out of their hair for a while."

I sank down beside her. "What don't they know? I don't understand."

Tuppence ambled over and laid her muzzle on Sheriff Marge's thigh.

Sheriff Marge absently stroked the hound's head. "Your mom. He was tracing her Mercedes. I didn't give him any help, but he's a smart guy. He'll find it tonight or tomorrow."

I inhaled. It was a lot to take in. "So her car's going to be repossessed? Why did he stop by the sheriff's office?"

"It's a courtesy the more reputable firms extend to local law enforcement—to let us know they'll be taking action in our jurisdiction."

"How much trouble is she in?" I whispered.

Sheriff Marge shrugged. "Nothing you imagined—no police reports, no arrests. I got whiffs of financial problems in my searches, though—a few accounts sent to collections." She turned to face me. "I've done all I can. Anything else you'll have to learn from her."

I nodded. "Thanks."

Mom brought out the ice cream sandwiches. I made mine last as long as possible, nibbling and licking down to the last smooshy morsel. I just wasn't up to faking pleasant conversation at the moment.

Then the California motor coaches pulled into their spots, and the crew emerged, giving us something to watch and postponing conversation even further. Doors slammed. People hollered at one another. Barbecues were ignited. From the savory smoke drifting our way, I'd say a few of the crew members knew about good food. Too bad Melvin hadn't asked for their help on the script.

I was debating whether or not to tell Sheriff Marge about the photos Mom had swiped from Vince's backpack when I caught the sound of my phone ringing from the trailer. I scooted off the bench and trotted to the RV.

Breathless, I picked up.

"Meredith? Meredith?" The woman's voice was frantic. "It's Barbara. Barbara Segreti."

"Are you okay?"

"I-I don't know. Yes, I think so. Yes. Yes, I am." Her voice got stronger the more she talked, but her repetitions didn't sound right to me.

"Barbara, what's happened?" I hopped off the fifth-wheel's steps and hurried toward the picnic table.

"They know," she whispered. "They know."

"Who knows?" I laid a hand on Sheriff Marge's shoulder and mouthed Barbara's name.

Sheriff Marge scooped a hand, indicating I should let her listen in. I bent my head near Sheriff Marge's and held the phone so we could both hear.

"The family. They know. They sent a message."

Sheriff Marge prompted me with a nod. "What kind of message?" I asked.

"They trashed my shop. It's all—it's all—" Barbara was breathing hard. I heard crunching, clinking noises in the background, as if she was stepping on broken glass, shoving things out of her way.

"Vandals?"

"No. The family."

She wasn't making sense. "Barbara, Sheriff Marge is here with me. We're coming over."

"No—no. We have to go to the museum—before it's too late."

"The Imogene?"

"Meet me at the back door to the basement." There was a thump, and the line went dead.

"Come on," Sheriff Marge grunted and pushed herself to standing. "I don't like the sound of that. Barbara's a sensible woman—not normal for her to get rattled."

Sheriff Marge's cast made it impossible for her to bend her knee. As a squat, solid person, her center of gravity is stable—and low. Mom and I tried, as delicately as we could, to heave Sheriff Marge into my pickup. We had to put our hands and elbows on places we wouldn't, normally—namely, Sheriff Marge's posterior.

Sheriff Marge spluttered, and clunked herself on the head with an errant crutch. Mom jerked the crutches out of the cab and tossed them in the pickup's bed in order to make room for herself on the bench seat. She ended up with Sheriff Marge's leg angled across her lap.

I ran around and squeezed behind the steering wheel.

"Hurry up." Sheriff Marge braced herself against the dashboard. "You can speed."

In my haste, I hit the giant pothole at the entrance to State Route 14. We all levitated briefly, then slammed back down onto the seat.

"Blast," Sheriff Marge muttered. She arched her back and reached a hand underneath her bottom, in the process squashing me against the driver's-side door. I swerved. She yanked her holster to the side. "Stupid gun belt."

I pulled the truck out of its fishtail wobble, and air seeped back into my lungs. "Where to?" I wheezed.

"Imogene's on the way. Check the parking lot first, but if she's not there yet, head to the Golden Shears. I don't like the idea of Barb alone at her shop if it's been damaged." Sheriff Marge smacked my knee. "Faster, girl. Go!"

I stomped on the accelerator, my hands taut white clamps on the steering wheel at the ten and two positions. My commute's short, thank God. The wheels chattered as I careened around the corner onto the access road to the county park, the marina, and the museum. We all slid left on the seat, and I ended up with the air smashed out of me again.

"Loop around back. Don't stop!" Sheriff Marge shouted.

I gunned the truck down the long parking lot, veered into the driveway reserved for deliveries, bounced off a curb, and shot into the tiny lot, mostly occupied by a large dumpster, behind the mansion. No other cars.

I threw the truck into reverse.

"Wait. Wait!" Mom yelled.

I glanced in the rearview mirror and slammed on the brakes. A white Toyota Corolla with rust spots on the hood screeched to a stop inches from my back bumper. Barbara.

We sat there shuddering for half a second.

"Out. Get out!" Sheriff Marge started thrashing her way toward the door.

Mom popped her door handle and just about fell out of the truck. She pulled, and I pushed, and Sheriff Marge slid off the seat, landing on her good foot. Mom retrieved the crutches and handed them over.

By the time we got ourselves together, Barbara was standing at the back door of the museum, wringing her hands.

I ran to Barbara, Sheriff Marge pedaling as fast as she could behind me while Mom fluttered around her, trying to help.

"Are you okay?" I touched Barbara's shoulder. She was trembling.

"I need to see." She pointed an unsteady finger at the lock on the door. "Inside. Hurry. Please."

I unlocked the door, pushed it open, and stepped back. Barbara rushed inside—in the dark. She seemed to know exactly where she was going.

I flipped on the light switches, and the long, cavernous room flickered into view. "Barbara?" I called.

She was hustling down the center aisle, her rubber-soled sneakers squeaking softly on the concrete floor. I trotted after her.

"Barbara?" I caught up with her at the right-hand turn into the laundry area, an odd chunk of the building that seemed to have been an architect's afterthought. But it was well equipped with massive washing machines, wringers, industrial dryers, presses, and several rolling carts for handling the huge quantities of table and bed linens the large Hagg family would dirty while on vacation.

Barbara headed straight for the anomaly in the room—an avocado-green washer-and-dryer set sized appropriately for a 1970s suburban split-level. I'd been meaning to get rid of them for a couple of years.

She lifted the lid on the washing machine and peered inside. Then she whirled around and pressed her hands against her chest, which was heaving. "It's here. It's still here."

CHAPTER 16

"What's still here?" I leaned over the washing machine. Inside, a bulky, crunched canvas roll was coiled in jerky angles around the center shaft. "Barbara, is this—?" My mouth was dry.

"I had to hide it somewhere. And I couldn't tell you because—for your safety. For everyone's safety. But they know . . ." Her voice trailed off in a whisper.

"Know what?" Sheriff Marge asked, puffing hard.

"Well, I don't know—exactly," Barbara said.

Sheriff Marge scowled at me. "Will someone explain, please?" Then she glanced around quickly. "I need to sit."

Mom ducked into the big room and returned dragging a wooden rocking chair. Sheriff Marge dropped into it.

"Let's get it out." I pulled and pinched and yanked. I finally swung a knee over the corner of the washing machine to get leverage for unwinding the unyielding canvas tube. "How'd you get it in here?" I grunted.

"I don't know. It wasn't this hard," Barbara panted, bumping shoulders with me as we heaved. "But I was racing on adrenaline. I had to find a place, fast." She took hold of the loose end while I reached back into the tub to wrangle the other end.

We lifted the canvas roll and flopped it on the large table originally used for folding clothing. My fingers itched at the edge of the roll, and I took a deep breath. The painting was probably irreparably damaged from its treatment. Acrylic paint retains some flexibility when dry, but not enough to withstand this much crimping, especially not with Cosmo's heavy hand. But I didn't care, did I? Why was I suddenly concerned about the condition of the most hideous painting I'd ever seen?

"Well?" Sheriff Marge creaked forward in the rocking chair.

I nodded and expelled my breath, cheeks puffing. Barbara helped me unroll the painting.

"Oh dear, oh dear," she murmured, hovering over the longest paint crack, which ran vertically down the end that had been at the center of the roll. "But I don't think Cosmo would mind." A feeble smile crossed her face. "It's not about the painting itself. It can't be. There's something else."

She was right. It was impossible for the painting to ascend to a new level of repulsiveness. It was already at the top of the ugliness spectrum.

"Is it about what's in the paint?" I asked.

"In?" Barbara's mouth pulled into a worried frown. "I thought maybe under, or behind—like a false back, but I didn't find any papers when I cut out the canvas." Her forehead wrinkled as she glanced up at me. "In?"

"Gold dust?"

Barbara drummed her fingers on the tabletop and slowly nodded. "I wouldn't put it past him."

"Details." Sheriff Marge stretched her leg into a more comfortable position and pulled a notebook from her chest pocket. "Want to fill me in?"

"First of all, how do you know Cosmo?" I asked.

"I don't—or didn't," Barbara said. "Not really. Just in the way all little kids know of their parents' adult acquaintances. Tall and intimidating and stern and just there sometimes. The 'Say hello to Mr. Hagg, Barbara; now run along and play' variety. Except sometimes Cosmo would slip me Necco wafers. He knew I favored the purple clove ones, and he saved them for me. I liked him for that."

Barbara plopped on the floor. With one hand, she massaged the back of her neck beneath her still-immaculate beehive. There was probably a pound of hairspray holding it together, which had to become even heavier throughout the day.

"It wasn't until my Dad died that Mom explained about our family's connection to the Mafia, and how Dad had begged to be released. I had just graduated from beauty school and was going to take over the barber shop. I think she finally thought it was safe to tell me." Barbara shook her head. "All those years, Dad was in exile here—the only safe way to leave the mob in those days was to get some higher-ups to pull strings and promise to stay out of the action in a very remote location and to keep your mouth shut. Even then, it wasn't a completely free pass. The barber shop and our little house became a rest stop of sorts for wiseguys needing to cool their heels for a while."

Barbara sighed, rolled her shoulders, and continued, "That's when I made the connection—Dad's many visitors and why they were visiting—"

"But Cosmo was a local boy," I interrupted. "And not Italian."

Barbara snorted. "They didn't care about your pedigree as long as you produced. A man had to be Italian—preferably Sicilian, on his father's side—to become a made man, but other than that, the mob was happy to collect their percentage from whatever racket you could come up with. I don't know the details because I just overheard snippets during poker games in the back room, but I got the impression Cosmo was always working on some scheme or other. He had connections in Los Angeles."

"So Cosmo was in the mob?" Sheriff Marge scratched behind her ear with the end of her pen.

"I think it's more likely the mob found out about his activities and suggested he share the proceeds with them. Under penalty of physical harm if he didn't." Barbara swept a few pieces of lint into a neat pile with her hand. "That's how they work—a finger in every pie, whack you if you don't comply. It results in a lot of pressure on low-level criminals to always be coming up with something new to meet the mob's demands for money."

"You think Cosmo was a low-level criminal?" Mom crossed the room and sat beside Barbara. She leaned against an industrial dryer and pressed her fingertips over her eyes.

"More like a one-hit wonder. He'd done something to make him a golden boy in the mob's eyes for a while, but it didn't last. I remember him brainstorming with Dad late into the night many times. He always seemed desperate for cash. For some reason, Dad had a soft spot for him and tried to help him."

"What does this have to do with the painting?" Sheriff Marge asked.

"Cosmo painted it at our house, in the spare room. He left it there and would come work on it every couple weeks. I was in high school at the time, and I remember how haggard he was. Something was dreadfully wrong, and it seemed as though he'd given up. He normally was mischievous, a jokester, but all the spark had gone out of him."

"When was that?" I blurted. "He died shortly after, right?"

Barbara nodded. "It was as though the painting was his masterpiece." She glanced at the table, where the curled ends of the canvas contradicted her. "Not that the work itself was good, but that, somehow, it was his best work. I guess I have a sentimental attachment to it. I always thought Cosmo led such a sad life, even though he forced a jolly exterior for the benefit of a little girl."

"Why steal—or hide—the painting?" I asked.

"I saw that filmmaker at the fundraiser, and I knew. They'd finally come." Barbara rose on one plump knee and pushed herself to standing. "Speaking of which, we have to get it out of here. They've searched my shop. Their next stop will be here." She turned to Sheriff Marge. "Can you lock it up?"

"Why?" Sheriff Marge snapped her notebook closed.

"It's Cosmo's revenge. I'm sure of it. I'm just not sure how—" Barbara hurried to the table and started rolling the painting back up. "But the mob has sent Juice's nephew to nab it. We can't let that happen. We can't." She worked fast, her arm flab jiggling with the effort.

Barbara hefted the roll in her arms, turned toward us, and let out an unearthly shriek.

The top of the roll, near her head, disintegrated in a puff of paint powder and canvas bits as a gunshot reverberated off the stainless-steel and concrete surfaces.

CHAPTER 17

Barbara hit the floor and rolled under the table. I'm embarrassed to say the rest of us were rooted to our spots for a couple nanoseconds while the idea that we were being shot at sank in.

The hot-water heater in the corner sprouted two neat, round leaks. I cringed and ducked—the racket was deafening. From my knees, I spun around and saw Vince—the big goon—standing directly behind Sheriff Marge's rocking chair, blocking the only doorway, his gun arm raised.

Another bullet thwanged off the barrel of the wringer next to Mom.

He might have the look of a mercenary, but he didn't have the skills—the guy was clearly not a good shot.

Click. Click—click. He also wasn't faithful about cleaning his weapon.

Vince swore and bent in half, hiking up the hem of his jeans. Rats. Rats. Rats. Saskia had underestimated him. He had a backup, fully loaded, ankle holster.

"Move!" I shouted. "Keep moving!"

Mom army-crawled toward Barbara. I scootched toward the stainless-steel double sink.

Sheriff Marge rocked like crazy. With her back toward the shooter and her bum leg, the best she could hope for was that he'd hit her Kevlar vest instead of her unprotected head. She was wrestling with her gun belt. It had all kinds of attachments—a walkie-talkie, flashlight, baton, Taser, other things I never want to meet the business end of—and several protuberances had wedged between the thin spindles under the chair's arms, effectively strapping her in the seat.

I reached the tin washtub stashed under the sink and started hurling its contents. Bristle brushes, tennis balls, spray bottles holding the dried remnants of green and blue liquids—anything to throw Vince off balance and give us time.

Vince dodged a darning egg and fired. His new gun aimed better, splintering off the corner of the table Mom and Barbara were huddled under. My hand hit the bottom of the washtub—I was out of ammunition.

I didn't see where the next bullet embedded, but Barbara screamed my name and held up a bloody hand. Mom was sprawled beside her, hair tangled over her face, not moving. I couldn't tell if her chest—*Was she breathing?*

Vince stomped on the back of one of Sheriff Marge's rockers, lurching her to a stop. "I'll take the painting now." He held out his free arm, indicating with an index finger that he wanted Barbara to bring it to him.

I glanced at Mom. She still hadn't moved. What had I gotten her into? I squeezed my eyes shut. I couldn't bear—I couldn't think about—

Blood rushed in my ears, louder than any gunshots. I may not like her much, probably because we're so alike, but she's still my mother. Nobody messes with my mother.

"I'll do it," I croaked.

Vince swung the gun in my direction as I rose to my feet. He glared at me for a moment, then gave a nod.

I squatted next to the table and reached for the painting.

"You can't. No. You can't," Barbara grunted as I tugged it from her grasp.

"I have to. Mom?" I whispered.

"I'm sorry, honey." Barbara blinked back tears. "I'm so sorry."

I walked slowly toward Vince. He must have seen me glancing at Sheriff Marge, because he stepped several feet to the side.

"Over here," he growled, panning his gun over both of us.

"Why do you want it?" I asked.

Out of the corner of my eye, I saw the end of Sheriff Marge's crutch slowly sliding in my direction. She eased her weight forward, bringing the chair to the forward tips of its rockers.

"None of your business. Hurry up." Vince motioned impatiently with the gun.

I sprang into a fast, extra-long stride. The crutch shot up, flipped against my shin, and I pitched forward spread-eagle. I got a face full of black T-shirt and rigid abs, and a gun went off.

Tumbling, I cracked against several rigid surfaces in sequence, elbows and knees smacking into cold, hard edges. More gunshots, too many to count—a pistol being unloaded in a nonstop barrage. I ended up plastered against the base of a washing machine at eye level with a floor drain, and on top of something rough and lumpy.

Everything was sideways and spinning and blurry and cold and bruised. I felt as though I'd been rolled through a wringer. A black-clad body wriggled toward me, arm outstretched.

Then two more pops, timed and calculated, and Vince stopped.

My breaths echoed in my head. But I concentrated on them—breathing is good, right?

Cold and hard. I drifted on an ice shard fog into a clammy abyss of concrete and stainless steel. I tried to swallow, but my tongue was too thick. Black and cold. I couldn't stop shivering.

I opened my eyes to a khaki form sliding across the floor on her bottom, pushing herself with one leg and dragging the other, talking into her radio at the same time, requesting an ambulance. She laid a hand on my forehead and pinned an eyelid back. "Meredith?"

The spreading pain in my thigh ignited. "Yeah," I groaned.

"Don't move," Sheriff Marge said. "You got hit. Straight through on the outside edge. You'll be fine."

"Mom?" I rasped.

"Right here." Mom's voice sounded far away, but she leaned into view, her auburn hair puddling on the floor. "It's all over." She laid down beside me, our faces even.

"I thought—you were—" I struggled to push up on my elbow.

Sheriff Marge shot out an arm and pinned me down. My legs were dead weights. I glanced down to find Barbara leaning on them with a towel twisted around my left thigh.

"Shhhh," Mom murmured. "Stunned. That's all. A flesh wound, same as you. See?" She pulled a wad of bloody fabric from her arm, revealing a nasty gash about three-quarters of the way from elbow to shoulder. "We match."

Her wobbly smile didn't convince me.

ooo

Mom made it to the ambulance under her own power and squeezed into a corner. I suffered the indignity of being strapped to the gurney and wheeled up the basement ramp. Sheriff Marge wedged in beside me, her cast taking up room for three. The paramedic sucked in his breath and latched the door. He couldn't even sit, just spent the jolting ride bent at the waist propping himself with a stiff arm against bins of medical supplies. He kept a wary eye on us.

Barbara followed in her little white car, with the painting belted into her passenger seat. Considering recent events, we weren't letting Cosmo's masterpiece out of our sight until we figured out why it was so coveted.

I craned my neck to a really uncomfortable angle to see Sheriff Marge. "What happened?"

"I tripped you."

"I know. I was hoping you would. But then?"

"I used the crutch to force that dumb rocking chair over, knocking me free." Sheriff Marge arched and pressed her fists into her lower back. Her gun belt was in a heap on her lap. She stretched her neck from side to side.

"You're going to be sore," Mom said.

"Already am," Sheriff Marge grunted. "What I get for not cinching up my belt. Think it worked loose while we were getting situated in your truck."

Mom stifled a giggle. "We must have looked like the Three Stooges bouncing off one another in our hurry to pile into the pickup." She giggled again, this time unsuppressed and too long, too high-pitched.

Sheriff Marge snorted and started bouncing on the seat. She lifted her glasses and wiped the corners of her eyes. "Blast this leg," she wheezed, giving her cast a slap, but she was chortling uncontrollably.

It hurt. I wrapped my arms around my stomach, the gurney straps cutting into my flesh—oh, it hurt. But I laughed until tears ran into my ears.

The paramedic shifted his supporting arm, his eyes narrowed. He appeared to be contemplating how to stab all of us with hypodermic sedatives at the same time. Or maybe he was wishing the ambulance came supplied with straitjackets. "You all need to settle down," he said in a gruff voice.

That just set us off again. Mom tittered, rocking forward and back in the corner. Sheriff Marge howled. I might have been cackling. A regular zoo.

But he needn't have worried. We exhausted ourselves to a limp lethargy by the time the ambulance arrived at the hospital.

The ER staff pulled me out, and Sheriff Marge hobbled beside me into the waiting area.

"There were two shots—at the end. Did you—?"

Sheriff Marge gave a brief nod. "He was crawling for you. His jammed gun was just behind your head. I couldn't let him—" She heaved a sigh. "He's dead."

"Thank you," I whispered. I raised my hand, and Sheriff Marge squeezed it.

A person in aqua scrubs and a shower cap pinched and poked me a few times, and I slipped into a warm, happy floatiness. No doubt I slurred and drooled and uttered mushy secrets, spilling my guts to whoever would listen—or not. Everyone seemed to be in an inexplicable rush while I took a magic carpet ride.

I knew Mom was in the next bed over, and I could see her whenever I wanted to—to make sure she was really okay. Then I think I slept for a long time.

ooo

Or maybe not. When I came to, the same bright fluorescent lights flickered overhead, and the same medical staff bustled around, their shoes squeaking and voices hushed.

I sat up and squeezed my eyes shut against the wave of dizziness that hit me. I inhaled and gripped the edges of the mattress with both hands. When I could look, I was glad to see I still had my own clothes on—on my top half, at least.

I pushed the heavy, heated blanket back. My left thigh was wrapped in puckered, taupe, stretchy tape.

"How're you doing?" Gemma materialized at my side. She stuffed a thermometer in my mouth so I couldn't answer.

"I think you're done with this." She ripped adhesive tape off the back of my wrist and removed the IV shunt.

When the thermometer beeped, I pulled it out of my mouth and handed it to her. "I thought you did OB and inpatient care."

Gemma blinked at me with those magnified green eyes behind her cat's-eye glasses. "Cross-training, hon. The staff here's so small, we all rotate. This is my week in ER. Lucky you." Gemma jerked her hair, perfectly sculpted in a 1960s flip, toward the opening in the hanging curtains. "At least she's not my patient this time."

Sheriff Marge sat in a vinyl visitor's chair in the hall with her leg outstretched, grousing into a cell phone. I caught enough of her conversation to realize she was complaining about a couple of her deputies' response times to our incident at the Imogene.

I ducked my head so she wouldn't catch me watching. She'd be able to read the guilty look on my face because I knew why her deputies were taking so long. I hoped our emergency hadn't prevented them from completing the job.

"You have a pressure bandage." Gemma brought me back to the issue at hand. "We'll get you an instruction sheet on how and when to change the dressings. And a prescription for painkillers."

"So I can go home?"

"You bet, hon. We don't admit for ticky-tacky injuries."

"Bullet wounds are ticky-tacky?" I glanced back down at my sausaged leg and frowned, wondering what it was going to feel like after the drugs wore off. For now, my thigh ached, tight and hot as though the muscles were burning after a challenging hike.

"It's all about location. Yours we could call liposuction."

"Thanks a lot."

Gemma's broad, starched white bosom jiggled at her own joke. "The bullet did actually slice through muscle, and you are bleeding— hence the pressure bandage. But you'll be fine."

"How's Mom?" I glanced at the next bed. Mom's head was deep in the pillow.

"We gave you both generous hits of morphine. She's still sawing logs. We'll let her wake up on her own."

Sheriff Marge huffed into the room followed by Barbara, who was pushing a chair with the canvas roll slumped in it.

"We need to talk," Sheriff Marge announced.

Barbara parked the chair, lifted the painting out, and laid it carefully across the end of my bed. It looked battered, with ratty edges and a large reddish-brown stain in the middle, plus a few deep indentations.

My stomach sank as my brain wrapped around the image. My blood. And the painting had been shot—those indentations were bullet holes all the way through the multiple layers of the roll.

Sheriff Marge sank into the chair, a frustrated scowl pushing her glasses low on her nose.

"I can take a hint," Gemma said. "But I'll be back in a few minutes to check on my other patient." She gave Sheriff Marge a pointed, no-nonsense look.

I grinned. Gemma doesn't take guff from anyone. A rare trait.

"Are you—do you have to be—what's the word? *Sidelined*?" I asked.

"Administrative leave," Sheriff Marge grumbled. "WSP will handle the investigation because my department's too small. No way my deputies could be unbiased with me hovering over them. But I can work on this." She jabbed a finger at the painting.

"I'm sorry," Barbara whispered. "I'm so sorry." Tears welled in her eyes.

"Don't be." I stretched out a hand, and she latched onto it as though it was her last hope. "You saved the painting, and whatever it represents." I pulled her against the side of the bed and wrapped an arm around her shoulders. She was warm and squashy, like a teddy bear. If it had been appropriate, I might have snuggled her. I was in need of some snuggling.

Actually, what I really needed was Pete. My heart hovered over that idea for a second before Barbara's words brought me back to reality.

"But you—and your mom." Barbara's tears were falling freely now. "I thought if I hid the painting, I would prevent people from getting hurt. He must have followed me. I lost my head when I found my shop ransacked. I led him straight to you."

"Are you sure?" I replied. "He could have followed us from the campground. Our departure wasn't exactly subtle—"

"No matter now," Sheriff Marge interrupted. "What matters is why. Why on earth is that disgusting painting worth killing for?"

"I have an idea," I said. "It's going to take a lot of acetone."

"Oh." Barbara's head jerked up in surprise. "Nail polish remover. I have gallons."

"Are you willing to donate them to a good cause?"

Barbara nodded, her eyes wide. She dabbed her cheeks with her sleeve.

I inhaled, making a checklist in my mind. "How long until the state patrol is finished processing the Imogene's laundry room?"

"Few hours, probably," Sheriff Marge said.

I glanced over at Mom's prone form. She was snoring softly—for real this time. "We'll be here for a while, too. As soon as we can, let's meet at the museum. We have some scrubbing to do."

CHAPTER 18

I must have dozed off again. I awoke to low laughter and found Gemma helping Mom slip her bandaged arm through the armhole in her blouse. The paramedics must have torn off the sleeve to treat her at the museum, so she looked like a proper little redneck in her cutoff muscle shirt.

"How are you?" Frankie leaned over the bed and squeezed my shoulder.

"Ready to get out of here."

"That's why I'm here. Sheriff Marge called. I'm your ride home." Frankie pursed her lips. "I've also been instructed to tell you to call Pete ASAP. Apparently he's been trying to reach you, and when you didn't answer for hours, he got worried and called Sheriff Marge. She gave me a lecture on your behalf about not being an answering service—or a matchmaking service." Frankie's brown eyes sparkled with amusement.

I patted the sheets around me. My phone's usually nearby. And then I remembered and groaned. "It's in my truck—at the museum."

"Use mine." Frankie dropped her phone in my lap and hurried around the bed to help Gemma situate Mom in a wheelchair.

I dialed Pete's number and closed my eyes, listening to the distant ringing.

"Frankie?" Pete's voice was scratchy, urgent. "Have you seen Meredith?"

"It's me," I whispered.

He was silent for a long time, just breathing. Finally, he said, "How bad?"

"Not. Not at all. Just a scratch," I said, staring at my swollen leg.

"That's not what Sheriff Marge said."

"She exaggerates."

An involuntary chuckle ripped from Pete's throat—because we both know that's the opposite of Sheriff Marge's personality. But he didn't say anything.

"I'm here," I murmured. "And I'll still be here when you get back."

"I'm counting on it." He sounded as though he was choking up. "I love you."

I leaned into the phone as if it was Pete himself. "I love you, too."

When I clicked off, Gemma was standing at my bedside, fists on hips, with one eyebrow arched over the thick rim of her glasses. "'Bout time the two of you got that settled," she said crisply, then nodded toward the wheelchair. "Your turn."

For the second time in twenty-four hours, Mom and I squeezed awkwardly into a pickup—this time Frankie's little new-to-her S-10. Mom perched sideways on the fold-down backseat and nested the painting at her feet so I could enjoy the leg room the passenger seat afforded.

Frankie delivered us to the fifth-wheel and stayed to tuck Mom and me in our respective beds, with water, pills, tissues, and whatever else we might need piled within arm's reach. She promised to return in a few hours, when it was daylight and I could somewhat politely roust a forensic art analyst from his slumber and beg his assistance.

OOO

The next morning, Frankie brought us maple bars and bottled apple juice from Junction General. My entire leg sensed every bump and jostle, magnifying it into shooting pain. The pressure bandage itched like crazy, and it was all I could do to keep from tearing it off. I popped the allowed dosage of Vicodin along with a swig of juice and hoped the resulting mental fuzziness would wear off by the time I needed to concentrate.

I hobbled gingerly down the trailer's steps, Frankie offering her shoulder as a hand grip and bearing much of my weight. On level ground, I maneuvered pretty adroitly, considering. Not gracefully, but I got where I wanted to go with only a few grimaces. Thank God for painkillers.

Mom's color had returned, and she'd applied her usual makeup. She'd pulled on a bulky sweater that masked the bandage on her arm and hitched her purse over the opposite shoulder. If I hadn't been at the hospital myself, I would never have guessed she'd spent the better part of the night in the ER.

Her face fell, though, when she caught sight of the empty spot next to my trailer—the place where her Mercedes had been parked. A crinkle appeared between her brows. She lowered her lashes, purposefully avoiding eye contact with me, and hurried to Frankie's pickup. Maybe she was hoping I hadn't noticed.

Frankie and I loaded a plastic kiddie pool I keep on hand to help Tuppence survive hot days into the pickup's bed.

When we got to the museum, I gave Mom the keys to unlock the basement door.

Frankie lingered at the passenger door, watching Mom walk away. "Meredith, I need to give you something," she said in a low voice. She leaned into the cab, clicked open the glove compartment, and pulled out a yellow sheet from a triplicate form. "This was stuck on your door last night. I pulled it off without thinking and shoved it in my purse.

This morning, when I found the paper again, I skimmed over it. I shouldn't have, I suppose. I'm sorry for intruding."

I took the page from her outstretched hand. A notice of repossession. Details about Mom's Mercedes were typed in the blanks—VIN number, year, model, color, as well as Mom's home address. The recovery agent had handwritten the address where the vehicle was seized, and scrawled his name and date.

"Is there anything I can do to help?" Frankie laid a protective hand over the huge agate pendant dangling from her necklace, a pinched look on her face.

I shook my head. "She won't even let me help—not yet anyway." I folded the paper and stuffed it in my bag. "Did you have this much difficulty with your mother?" I meant it as a rhetorical question, but Frankie sighed.

"Oh, yes." Her helmet hair bobbed emphatically. "Even up to the day she died, I was terrified of disappointing her. She was the icon of perfection, and I never measured up. In a way, I'm glad I don't have children, especially not a daughter. At least no one has to deal with that kind of treatment from me. It seems inevitable that those expectations get passed along from generation to generation, although I don't think my mother meant to inflict emotional pressure."

Barbara drove up and parked between my truck and Frankie's. Shades of last night, but we were more orderly today. Sheriff Marge sat lengthwise on Barbara's backseat, being chauffeured in style.

"Here, let me." Frankie took over management of the kiddie pool.

Barbara opened her trunk, revealing several cardboard boxes.

"Frankie will show you where the hand truck is," I said.

Barbara nodded, and bustled toward the museum in Frankie's wake.

"Now you know what it feels like," Sheriff Marge grunted, "not being able to do things for yourself. Being coddled."

"Yuck." I extended my hand and helped Sheriff Marge scoot off the seat and stand upright.

She wedged the crutches under her armpits and fixed a stern gray gaze on me. "Ready?"

So she *had* noticed that I was reluctant to enter the Imogene's basement. I shrugged.

"The sooner you deal with it, the better."

"You've done this before." I limped beside her, our pace blessedly slow.

"Unfortunately, yeah." She stopped and shoved her glasses up with a forefinger before peering up at me, still over the top of the lenses. "I've never fired in anger—at least not yet. So my conscience is clear in that regard. The three men I've killed, I did so in order to prevent them from harming or killing someone else. It's hard to read a person's intent—so sometimes you wonder. But Vince wasn't trying to wing people, Meredith. He'd established a pattern of violence in a very short time, and there was no way I could let him get ahold of that gun, not so near to you."

I bit my lip and nodded, glancing away to blink tears out of my eyes.

Sheriff Marge nudged me with her elbow. "I like having you around. I suspect there are quite a few people who share my opinion. Speaking of which—" Her voice lowered from contemplative to the no-nonsense timbre, her eyes narrowed. I couldn't tell if she was irritated or secretly amused. "You did call Pete back, didn't you? That man was driving me crazy with pestering." She snorted and resumed her swinging, stumping gait.

The laundry room was in disarray. Apparently the state patrol does not include housecleaning in their forensic evidence collection service. Frankie hauled the pieces of the broken rocking chair out to the dumpster, while Barbara cleared off the table and picked up all the items I'd flung at Vince last night. We all tried to pretend there weren't puddles of dried blood on the floor even as we took creative side steps and shuffles to avoid them, like some kind of awkward dance.

Some of that blood wasn't mine. But it looked the same—the same thick, dark, rust-brown drips and smears. I shuddered and reminded myself that Vince had been willing—and able—to kill me. I replayed Sheriff Marge's words and took a deep breath. Busy—I needed to stay busy.

I splurged on the luxury of riding the elevator instead of climbing three flights of stairs to retrieve my laptop from my office. I didn't wake up Leland Smiley as I'd feared I would. He graciously claimed he was already on his second cup of tea, although his voice still held hints of early-morning frogginess.

When I'd explained our recent developments, Leland jumped into action, directing me to his Skype account and giving me a list of tools and supplies to assemble. Back in the laundry room, I set the laptop up on the corner of a washing machine so Leland could have a good view through the webcam.

Frankie stood on a chair and opened the two small windows that were above ground level. Barbara helped her prop oscillating fans on the ledges, and Mom plugged in a big box fan and set it in the doorway, aimed out into the basement. We'd be working in a windstorm, but it was a better option than passing out or risking a flash fire from the fumes.

We lifted the kiddie pool onto the table and unfurled the painting faceup in the big plastic tub. It was too big to lie flat, and it rippled in the bottom like wave-washed sand. Really ugly sand.

I turned on the laptop and connected with Leland. He must have been leaning into his video camera, because his face loomed on the monitor, all nose and chin and independent-minded bushy white eyebrows.

"Good morning," I shouted over the fans. "This is Frankie, Barbara, and my mother, Pamela." I pointed in turn to each of the women standing around the table wearing bright-yellow rubber gloves that reached their elbows and stiff waterproof aprons. "Also, our sheriff, Marge

Stettler." I turned the laptop so he could see Sheriff Marge resting on a low ottoman upholstered in psychedelic fabric featuring puce pineapples and fleurs-de-lis. Over the years, the mansion has experienced its share of truly awful home decorating concepts, the remnants of which have accumulated in the basement.

"Ladies," Leland said, "you have a big job ahead of you. Ready?" He rubbed his hands together in front of the camera. I'm sure he would have preferred to join us in person.

We followed his instructions, emptying gallon after gallon of Barbara's nail polish remover into the kiddie pool until the canvas was submerged. Leland provided a running educational commentary while we went to work with stiff brushes. In a more sensitive case, where the painting was of value, we would have needed to use pure acetone and spot-treat the canvas. But since our goal was to remove all the paint and dissolve it into a liquid slurry, the extra ingredients in the nail polish remover didn't matter.

The paint was forty years dry and stubborn. The motion Leland had us use was like currying a horse, and my arm muscles let me know they didn't appreciate the unusual exertion. Sweat dripped off my forehead, and my thigh throbbed under the pressure bandage. I leaned hard against the table, trying to transfer most of my weight to my good leg.

I glanced at Mom, who was scrubbing one-armed. She held her injured arm snug across her body. I leaned near her ear. "Want to take a break?"

"No way," she shot back. "This is too exciting."

The clump of tangled fishing line Cosmo had glued to the painting floated by. I scooped it out, gently shook it free of droplets, and set it on a pad of paper towels we'd laid under the table.

The acetone bath was turning murky. I ran my gloved fingers over the surface of the painting, applying a putty knife to the biggest paint clumps.

Leland's monologue dwindled. It had to be boring watching the backsides of four women huddled over a kiddie pool.

"Should I call you back when we're finished?" I hollered, looking up to catch his eye on the camera.

"No, no, no. I wouldn't miss this for the world. But I am going to nip out for more tea." He stood and sidestepped off the screen, leaving his empty chair spinning.

"Barbara," Sheriff Marge shouted, "I'm still trying to figure it out— how'd you smuggle the painting down here?"

Barbara extended her lower lip and blew at a few wisps of hair that had come loose from her beehive and were floating about her face. "Laundry chute. I couldn't drag that huge roll through the crowd of guests at the fundraiser. Then I hurried down the servants' stairwell and pulled it out of the cart." She nodded toward the big spring-loaded canvas cart that we had shoved aside.

The cart is normally positioned under the laundry chute as a safety measure. If someone fell down the chute, it would act as a sort of stiff trampoline, absorbing much of the impact. The freefalling daredevil would be banged and bruised up but would likely survive the fall, as I knew firsthand.

"Meredith almost caught me coming back up. Do you remember?" Barbara added.

I frowned. "That evening's a bit of a blur for me. I was frantic after I saw the empty frame."

"I'm sorry. But now you know—" Barbara's eyes drifted to the biggest bloodstain on the floor. "I thought for sure you'd notice I was panting and sweating from dashing up the basement stairs. I did the first thing I could think of—ask about your hair."

I chuckled. "It worked. But how did you know about the laundry chute? We don't advertise its presence because it's such a hazard."

An impish grin spread across Barbara's face. "I grew up here— remember? Rupert and I used to spend hours playing hide-and-seek in

147

this old place. I know all its nooks and crannies. I just don't fit in most of them anymore."

"Wow. I guess I just didn't think—" I shook my head.

"That Rupert and I were kids once? I was a year behind him in school." Barbara's face turned wistful, and the way she said Rupert's name triggered a little bell in my head. Hmm.

"Oh!" Mom said. She started patting the bottom of the kiddie pool. "I just felt—there it is." She pulled a clenched gloved fist out of the mucky liquid and opened her hand, palm up.

A dull brass key.

"What?" Sheriff Marge heaved herself up on her crutches and crowded in beside me.

I glanced around our group. We were all holding our breath. I hated to disappoint them. "Not quite what I was expecting."

Mom dropped the key into my hand, and I rubbed it hard with my thumb.

"There's engraving on the bow—hand-done, though, and faint." I squinted at the key, then up at the circle of anxious ladies. "I have a magnifying glass in my office."

"Go ahead," Sheriff Marge said. "I'll take your place here." She propped herself against the table and gestured for me to hand over my rubber gloves.

"What were you expecting?" Frankie asked.

"Gold dust." Leland answered for me from the laptop. "It's there. I'm sure of it. Sprinkled onto the wet layers of paint, then painted over and over again."

"So that's why it was so thick." Mom's eyes were wide.

"And to hide this." I held up the key. "Probably under that wad of fishing line."

"Gold?" Barbara stared at her hands submerged in the dirty bath, glanced up at me with an excited smile, then resumed scrubbing with vigor.

CHAPTER 19

I set up the clamp-on magnifying glass and sank into my office chair. I pulled over the trash can and propped my leg up, releasing a hefty sigh. The sight of my monstrously swollen ankle made me wince. Actually, I didn't have an ankle—my entire leg was puffed to the point of having no contours—just a log in a hideous shade of yellowish lavender with a shoe at the end.

A skirt was the only thing I'd been able to wear on my lower half today, but that meant everyone was treated to a view of my sickening misshapenness. Ugh. Vanity—all is vanity.

I clicked on the lamp and held the key under the magnifying glass. If I tilted it just right, scratchy letters appeared—and a number. I grabbed a pad of paper and a pencil and wrote: *Astoria Vault & Trust #109.*

Astoria. There are a lot of Astorias in the United States, but I had a sinking feeling I knew which Astoria this was—Astoria, Oregon, where Cosmo had been swept overboard off a chartered fishing boat and drowned.

I fired up the cranky old PC and did an Internet search. The only bank in Astoria that wasn't part of a regional or national chain was

Astoria Trust and Loan. Not exactly the same name, but worth a phone call. Maybe Cosmo had abbreviated when etching the key, or maybe the bank's name had changed sometime in the past forty years.

When a pleasant-voiced woman answered, I explained my problem.

"Astoria Vault & Trust? You need to talk to Selwyn," she said. "One moment."

There followed ten minutes of inane elevator music, which gave me plenty of time to contemplate Cosmo's vagaries. He certainly upheld the Hagg family tradition of eccentricity. What was he up to—posthumously?

Finally, a click and a "Hello?"

"Yes." I straightened quickly. "Selwyn?"

He chuckled. "That's me. Selwyn Ferguson at your service."

"I've just found a key, hand-etched. It says Astoria Vault & Trust #109. Do you know what it might be for?"

"Number 109, you say? At last." His mellow tenor voice trembled.

"At last?"

"We only have three occupied boxes left, and 109 is one of them. It's been five years since the contents of any boxes were retrieved. That year we found two key-bearers. We're making progress." He sounded genuinely excited.

What kind of business was he in that having a customer every five years was good news? "What do I do with the key?"

"Bring it in, of course. As soon as possible."

"It's Thursday," I murmured, thinking through my schedule.

"We're open until five o'clock." Selwyn panted into the phone. "I could arrange to stay late if I know you're coming."

"Today?" Why was he so eager?

My phone emitted the soft buzz that I had another call. "Can you hold?" I punched a button.

"Meredith?"

I smiled at the accent. "Maurice. Thanks so much for your information. I haven't heard yet about the results, but I know the sheriff's department executed a search warrant on the Lamborghini owner's property last night."

"Awesome." I could hear the grin in his voice. "I'm outside."

"What?"

"The sign says the museum should be open by now, but the doors are locked."

"Oh." I checked my watch to verify—11:14 a.m. Late because my staff of one was up to her elbows in acetone in the basement. "You're here—in your fast car?"

"That's the only way I roll, sweetheart. You going to let me in?"

"I'll be right down." I switched over to Selwyn. "I have an idea. I may be able to make it today. Are you at the same location as Astoria Trust and Loan?"

"Yes, yes, the embarrassing stepchild in the basement."

"If it works out, I'll call you from the road to let you know my estimated time of arrival." I clicked off and hobbled to the elevator.

OOO

"What happened to you?" Gentleman that he was, Maurice was trying not to stare, but frankly, my leg was an eye-magnet. There's nothing quite like grossing out a nice man with a fast car.

"Bullet wound. Nothing serious."

"Bullet—serious?" Maurice spluttered. "You should be lying down—sitting, at the least." He grasped my elbow and ushered me into the gift shop.

"Ooof." I braced a hand against the counter as he boosted me up on the stool behind the cash register. "Really, I'm fine."

"This will not do." Maurice snatched an embroidered cushion that read OLD FISHERMEN DON'T DIE, THEY JUST SMELL THAT WAY from a display rack, knelt on one knee, and scooped up my leg, resting my ankle on top of the pillow on his other knee. He frowned up at me, his mustache angled down.

Talk about awkward. If I kept looking at him, I was going to burst out laughing. I quickly picked up the manila envelope he'd tossed on the counter. "You brought back the canvas strips."

"Leland said you'd want them. Something about metal traces."

"Right." I'd add them to the acetone soup downstairs. "Remember that ride you offered me?"

"I was hoping you'd bring that up." Maurice grinned, revealing a row of neat, even teeth below the mustache, and a rosy lower lip.

"How do you feel about Astoria? Now?" I bit the inside of my cheek, trying not to show him how anxious I was. It's at least a three-hour drive, one way. With rush hour on the edge of Portland, it could be much more. "I need to get to a bank before they close."

"Giving me a challenge, sweetheart? Say no more."

I filled in the ladies and Leland. We made the executive decision to keep the museum closed for the day since we had more pressing matters to attend to. Frankie, Barbara, Mom, and even Sheriff Marge trooped outside to help me slide into Maurice's passenger seat underneath the wing door and see us off.

Maurice wore driving gloves, and the machine rose rapidly through her gears. I felt sucked backward into the low recumbent seat. Maurice had such a determined look of fierce concentration on his face that I didn't think conversation was a good idea. And the scenery, which I normally enjoy, flew past so quickly that I was getting sick to my stomach. Between my next dose of Vicodin, my lack of sleep the night before, and the engine's droning, guttural vibrations, the moment I closed my eyes, I dropped off.

I awoke in a haze to Maurice patting my shoulder. "I'm just filling up, sweetheart. You comfortable?"

"Apparently," I mumbled.

His door whooshed open, and he climbed out. The blast of fresh air woke me the rest of the way, and I gasped, remembering. I checked my watch and peered out the window trying to peg our location.

An Alaska narrow-bodied commuter plane with a smiling Eskimo face painted on the tail roared overhead, wheels down—probably packed with the several-times-per-day busload of passengers from Seattle or Victoria or Twin Falls. Which meant we were near Portland International Airport.

I pulled out my phone and dialed the number for Astoria Trust and Loan. This time, Selwyn came on the line almost immediately.

"We should arrive between three thirty and four o'clock," I said.

"Hmm, 109, 109," he chanted, sounding gleeful. "I shall be ready. Do you have a case to transport the contents of the box?"

"Oh," I said, startled, "I'd been thinking along the lines of a will or maybe a handful of papers."

"Box 109 is one of our largest. I've never seen the contents, of course, but for John Smith to rent a box that size usually means—"

"John Smith?"

Selwyn chuckled. "No one ever used their real names, not for this sort of thing. At one time I had fourteen John Smiths on record. You'd think they could be a little more creative. If you have the key that fits the lock, then the contents of the box are yours. We don't ask questions."

"How big?"

Selwyn considered for a moment. "Don't you worry, dear. I'll make arrangements here so you won't have a delay. See you in a couple hours."

Now I was certain Cosmo was—had been—certifiably crazy. Why couldn't he have left a nice will and stash of bond certificates with his lawyer? It was as though he'd set up a scavenger hunt for his descendants—and by proxy, me. I glanced over my shoulder. The LaFerrari didn't appear to have a trunk.

CHAPTER 20

When we reached Astoria and found the stalwart granite bulk of Astoria Trust and Loan, Maurice had to heft me out of the passenger seat. My swollen leg had stiffened into a semi-bent position.

I hopped around on my good leg, moaning, as blood filtered back into my veins, throbbing as it did so. "Ow, ow, ow," I panted.

"You really ought to be in bed," Maurice pointed out.

I gritted a grimace that was supposed to be a smile but probably had nothing pleasant about it. "Tomorrow." I grabbed the handrail and did a single-step-at-a-time shuffle up the steep stairs that rose like a pyramid to the bank's impressive entrance. Because I'm classy like that—and I wasn't about to ask Maurice to carry me.

A lady behind a desk—a loan officer—took one look at Maurice and me and hurried over. I think she probably wanted to stash us—the circus strong man and the deformed woman—in a private office as quickly as possible to keep our sideshow from scaring off the other patrons. Either that or shoo us back out the door.

"Selwyn Ferguson?" I blurted.

The lady froze. "Oh. You're—" Her eyes darted between Maurice and me. "Yes, well. That makes sense. If you'll take the elevator to the basement?" She pointed to a set of burnished brass doors in the far corner of the bank's marble cavern of a foyer.

Maurice cocked his head at me.

I nodded and tossed a "Thank you" to the lady over my shoulder.

"This place is solid," Maurice muttered once we were enclosed in the plush elevator. The doors sealed like an airlock, and a quiet hum indicated we were descending. "And old. Feels nefarious, doesn't it?" He winked at me. "The underbelly of commerce, eh?"

He made me laugh. "You might not be that far off. Did Leland tell you his suspicions about the painting?"

"Nope. And I don't want to know. I stick to cars. He does art."

"I might be committing a crime. I'm not sure."

Maurice shoved his hands in his pockets and rose to his tiptoes. "So I'm your getaway driver?" He grinned wide. "That's fine by me, sweetheart. Just tell me where you need to go." He pulled a theatrical frown for a second and stared down at me. "A crime of passion?"

I chuckled. "A crime of nosiness. Poking about in other people's business because I have the key."

"Sounds like fun." Maurice held the doors open as I hobbled out into a cool, dank room.

I wouldn't have been surprised if the walls were coated in condensation. It felt as if we were a long ways underground—a complete absence of sound except Maurice's recent comment, which was still bouncing around the empty room.

"Ms. Morehouse? If I may call you Meredith?"

I jumped and searched, squinting in the dim lighting, for the voice's source. A rail-thin, stooped man shuffled softly into sight. His shock of bright white hair gleamed in the dusky shadows. He held his hands out in front of his body slightly, exposing white shirt cuffs from the end of his jacket sleeves. He'd sounded much younger on the phone.

"Mr. Ferguson? Selwyn?"

He came to a halt a few feet in front of me and straightened, casting his eyes in my direction, and I suddenly realized why he soft-stepped heel to toe, why he felt with his hands—he was blind. His irises swirled pale blue with no pupils, as though his lenses were coated with cataracts, although I had a hunch his blindness wasn't age related. He had the sure and practiced air of someone who'd successfully dealt with his handicap for a lifetime.

"Selwyn." I reached out and touched his hand.

He grasped mine firmly and held it, his skin papery and cool. "Ah. You're a brunette, very pretty. I'm sorry about your leg injury. You'll heal soon?"

My mouth fell open. Then I laughed. "I bet you say that to all the girls."

Selwyn chuckled and tucked my hand under his elbow. "Come with me. Your friend can wait here."

I shrugged back to Maurice. He nodded and leaned against the wall with his legs and arms crossed as though prepared to spend hours. The room was devoid of furniture or magazines to make his intermission more comfortable.

"It's a little game I like to play," Selwyn continued. "Was I right?"

"Yes—mostly. The pretty part's arguable. How'd you know my hair color?"

"Lucky guess. But I could tell from your footsteps that you're favoring a leg. And now I can feel it, too. I have an eidetic memory, but since I can't see, I file people by voices and scents." Selwyn guided me down a narrow, descending hallway. The air grew colder with each step.

"So this John Smith who rented box 109, how would you describe him?" I asked.

"Largish, portly. I can feel how much space a person takes up. Deep, gravelly voice, familiar with the local area, but I'd say he'd spent some time in Orange County or Los Angeles because there was a slight sharpening of the hard consonants and laziness in the vowels. He was more hurried than most Northwest natives. Smelled faintly of dry-cleaning fluid and a powder-coated candy—I'd say Necco wafers."

"Wow," I breathed.

"So he's your John Smith?"

I nodded, then remembered Selwyn couldn't see me. "Yes. Why here? This isn't a safe deposit box, is it? Even though we're in a bank."

Selwyn chuckled again. "Astoria Vault & Trust was here long before the bank was. They liked our building and the security the façade implies, and they infringed upon our name in order to piggyback on our reputation. Our business was decreasing, so it made sense to sell the facility. But we required them to lease the vault storage area back to us so we could maintain our contracts with our clients. They had a new vault installed for their needs."

"We?"

"My twin brother and I, our father before us, our grandfather before him, and our great-grandfather before him. All blind. It's a con-genital defect that's proven useful in this line of business. Back when Astoria was a booming shipping and fishing town, many seafaring men needed to store their valuables while they were gone for long periods of time. Often they wouldn't want those valuables to fall into the hands of their families or loved ones upon their deaths, for various reasons. Or when they returned from trips abroad, they might bring home items that again, for various reasons, shouldn't become public knowledge. We provided them security and anonymity."

Selwyn stopped and pivoted to the right. He pushed open a creak-ing wood door with huge wrought iron hinges. It felt as though we were in the dungeon of a medieval castle.

"Perfectly legal when the business originated," he continued, "but the laws have changed many times since then, and we're operating in a sketchy gray area. We haven't accepted new clients in a couple decades, but we're still honor bound to provide the service we contracted to existing clients."

We stepped into another dim room, this one equipped with a heavy wood table and two simple chairs in the center.

"My John Smith hasn't paid his rental fee in forty years."

"He prepaid. One hundred years," Selwyn answered.

I gasped. "One hundred years?"

"The longest term we offered. It was the renter's responsibility to take care of their two keys or pass them along to trusted people for safekeeping. Whoever has a key can open the box. If no one retrieves the contents by the end of the term, we are permitted to drill the box and keep the contents—if we want to."

"What treasures you must have."

"Not really. You'd be surprised at what other people think is valuable." Selwyn expertly ushered me around the table and through a second, incredibly thick, open door into a room covered floor to ceiling on all sides with cubbyholes ranging from standard mail slot to double-wide file-drawer size. The doors to nearly all the cubbyholes hung open, exposing black, empty interiors.

I thought back to Cosmo's grotesque painting and smiled. "It is a matter of taste."

Selwyn pointed to the lower-left corner at floor level, where a two-foot-square door was still closed. "There's 109. Try your key. You can remove the box inside and use the table in the anteroom to review the contents. I'll wait in the hallway so you have privacy. Call when you're ready." He released my arm and padded away.

I fished the key out of my purse and bent in half. Kneeling was out of the question. With blood rushing into my head and thumping in my ears, I fiddled with the lock. It took a fair bit of muscle, but the key finally turned.

The door swung open silently. A wood box with a handhold hole rested inside. I slid it out and clunked it on the floor. There was no way I could carry it in my condition—it had to weigh close to fifty pounds.

I stumped to the anteroom, dropped my purse on the table, and dragged a chair back into the vault. I gritted my teeth against the pain and hoisted the box onto the chair seat. After leaning against the chair back for a few minutes, panting, I towed the chair into the anteroom, its legs scraping grooves in the floor wax.

"Everything all right in there?" Selwyn called from the hallway, his voice wavering.

"So far."

My thigh pounded in pain under the pressure bandage. I pulled the second chair beside the first and dropped onto it, propping my leg up.

The box didn't appear to have a locking mechanism, just a simple clasp that popped open with light pressure. I removed the lid and nearly dropped it.

In half the box, stacks of banded hundred-dollar bills stared back at me. The other half held a jumble of small, thong-tied leather pouches, their folds crazed with age, and a sheaf of yellowed papers.

Rackets. Hadn't Rupert used that word when describing Cosmo's form of employment? I was pretty sure I was looking at a whole lot of ill-gotten gain. But by donating his painting—and the key intentionally hidden in the paint—to the Imogene, hadn't Cosmo also donated the contents of the box?

I exhaled. This was not a matter for me to decide. I didn't know what time it was in Ireland, but Rupert needed to know as soon as possible. I thumbed buttons on my phone, but there was no reception in the insulated depths of the vault.

I didn't even want to count the money. I lifted out pack after pack, scanning the series numbers on the top bills—late 1960s and early 1970s. There'd be very few bills that old in circulation anymore. The edges of the packs ruffled unevenly, the bills dingy and worn—so the money probably wasn't from a bank or treasury heist. They looked like they'd been fondled and tallied by someone not terribly tidy.

Inflation had taken its toll. The bills were worth a lot less than they had been when Cosmo stashed them away. Nonetheless, it was an astronomical amount of money—at least to me.

I picked at the knot in a leather thong securing a pouch, and bits crumbled into my hand. Carefully, I spread the pouch open, revealing a pile of dull, grainy powder, like coarse beach sand.

But not sand. Gold dust.

I did count the pouches—twenty-three.

The papers were newspaper clippings about the exploits and nominal jail sentences of several Los Angeles gangsters. Both Sam "Juice" Junkerman and Charles "Gnocchi" Nervetti were named as possible associates of the convicted wiseguys. Photos showed them dapper on courthouse steps beside equally well-dressed lawyers, smiles broad and cigars clamped between their lips. Cosmo sure knew how to pick his friends.

I fingered a stack of bills. Was this cache his revenge—or his getaway fund? Barbara had mentioned that Cosmo came to her father for advice—her father, who had semi-escaped the mob.

"Selwyn?" I called. "When was this box rented?"

"Friday, October 5, 1973," he answered. Gotta love that memory.

The month before Cosmo donated the painting—plenty of time to stick one of the keys into wet acrylic and paint over it until it held fast.

"Did John Smith ever come back and access his box again?"

"Once. Friday, April 12, 1974."

Friday. The day before Cosmo died.

"Did he come alone?"

"Yes, both visits."

"The second time, did he mention a chartered fishing trip planned for the next day?"

"Yes. Not eagerly, as most do. I got the impression he was under some obligation to show a couple business associates a good time. The deep-sea version of golf, good for deal-making."

Or unsuspected murder. How easy is it for someone to fall off a boat, especially if they get a nudge in the right direction and a billy club or gaff to the head? It could have been staged well enough that they might not even have had to pay off the charter captain, although that was a possibility, too. Where was the other key? Maybe at the bottom of the Pacific.

I roused myself from the morbid mental spiral with a deep sigh. "Selwyn, you mentioned a case for carrying these items. I'm going to need it. Or maybe two to distribute the weight—whatever you have."

CHAPTER 21

Maurice relieved Selwyn of the army-surplus duffel bags at the elevator. He tucked them under my feet and knees in the LaFerrari, giving me a footrest and support for my leg.

"Worthwhile?" he asked once he was strapped in beside me.

I nodded slowly. "Thanks for your help."

Maurice whistled a cheerful tune and eased the car out of the parallel curb spot.

I shifted against the uneasy sensation of a pile of cash cushioning me from the hot pavement we were skimming over. Plus, the gold—a better hedge against inflation than printed money, and in dust form, which isn't traceable, as opposed to stamped bars. Cosmo had been planning something—saving for an uncertain future, at the very least.

I dialed Rupert's number and left a cryptic message about needing to return my call as soon as possible. I insisted he try Frankie if he couldn't reach me because sleep was crashing down on my body again. She'd be able to tell him about the key and the gold dust buried in the still life's paint layers that hinted at so much more. My eyes drooped closed by the time I clicked off.

Maurice is an awfully good sport. He woke me up a few miles from the Imogene, giving me time to run my fingers through my hair and wipe the sleep from my eyes. I slid my tongue over my teeth—gross.

"Was I drooling?" I mumbled.

"Nope. Not a peep out of you. What kind of drugs are you on, sweetheart?"

"The good kind."

He braked and piloted the car onto the access road toward the marina and county park. He coasted to a stop in front of the museum, next to a black BMW I thought looked familiar. Maurice pressed a button, and my door swung upward. I felt as though I was about to be ejected from a time capsule back into the real world.

Maurice bounded around the car and scooped an arm under my shoulders to lift me out. Once on my feet, a bit wobbly but upright, I spotted the astonished face of my stepfather through the driver's window of the BMW.

Alex popped his door open and stepped out. "Meredith?" His eyes darted over me, taking in my purple swollen leg; Maurice, who was muscling the duffel bags out of the car; and the gull-winged, bright-red LaFerrari. I was sure he was getting the wrong impression.

"Alex." I tried to smile.

He enclosed me in an awkward hug. "Your mother called."

"About time," I muttered.

"She said you'd been shot—both of you." Alex kept his arm around my waist and ventured another look down at my leg. "You should be resting."

Alex had changed since I'd seen him last. He'd eschewed the comb-over and was sporting a respectable short fringe above his ears. Perfectly tailored charcoal pinstripe suit and conservative maroon tie, black wing-tips, as always, but he seemed softer, gentler, somehow. New wrinkles at the corners of his mouth. Paler, and maybe thinner under the suit.

"The doors are locked," he said. "I've been trying to reach your mother since I arrived, but she's not answering."

"She's probably still in the basement and can't hear her phone." I fished the museum keys from my purse. "I'll let you in. This is Maurice Banks."

Maurice shifted a bag so he held both duffels in his left hand and extended his right hand toward Alex. "G'day, mate."

I let Maurice get a head start along the sidewalk, then whispered to Alex, "Did Mom tell you about the Mercedes getting repossessed?"

He shifted his hold on me to help me step up on the curb. "There's more you need to know. We'll have a family conversation later."

I groaned inwardly. Family conversations were never pleasant episodes. Maybe I preferred living in frustratingly ignorant bliss.

Maurice dropped the bags inside the front door. "I have to hit the road—need to be back in Portland tonight." He bussed my cheek, then hovered near my ear. "You ever need anything, you'll let me know?"

"I still owe you dinner."

"Rain check, sweetheart. I'll be back."

Waving, I watched Maurice depart until he was a red blur between the trees.

Alex coughed. "I thought—isn't there a—I thought his name was Pete—um, out here? A friend of yours?"

I bit my lip and ducked my head to hide a smile. "Maurice is a friend. Pete is much more." I sighed and hefted a duffel bag. "If you stay a couple days, you'll get to meet him." Oh, goody. We were having a regular family reunion.

There really wasn't any point in taking the duffel bags to the basement because the Imogene doesn't have a decent safe, but I wasn't letting them out of my sight, either. Mom didn't seem surprised to see Alex. She rose from the ottoman, where she and Sheriff Marge had been propping each other up, shoulder to shoulder, and walked over to him, tipping up a cheek for him to kiss—their usual greeting. Alex went through the motions without animosity, and he kept his arms around her.

Barbara and Frankie were hunched over the deep sink, water splashing around them onto the floor.

"Meredith," Frankie squealed over her shoulder, "look at this." She and Barbara held up glass bowls, each with a couple of inches of the grainy sand in the bottom under clear, sloshing water.

"It was like panning for gold," Barbara said. "Leland just signed off a few minutes ago, once he was sure we weren't going to wash the dust down the drain." She giggled and wiped her forehead on a bare patch of skin above her rubber glove. "I'm exhausted, but I think we got it all. How about you? What did you find at the bank?"

"Did Rupert call?" I asked.

Frankie snapped off her gloves, draped them over the edge of the sink, and shook her head.

I frowned. "I left him an urgent message."

"He's probably on a plane or in an airport and can't use his phone." Frankie removed her apron and adjusted her cardigan, straightening the buttons along the front. "I called him last night after—" Her eyes drifted over my leg. "You should sit down."

Alex jumped into action and carted in a wood crate from the storage area under the stairs. I sank onto it, stretching my leg out in front of me. Sheriff Marge and I could have been twins except I was more colorful.

"Why is Rupert flying? I thought he was staying in Ireland for at least a week."

"He's coming home." Frankie pressed her lips together. "I know you don't think it's a big deal, but he needed to know you'd been shot. I told him. He caught the first flight home and should be here soon."

"So, the bank?" Sheriff Marge urged. She had deep circles under her eyes, and her hair stood up as though she'd been running her hands through it.

"The painting was just a hint. Barbara, I think the honor is yours."
I pointed to the duffel bags.

Barbara cast me a wondering look and squatted next to a bag. She
unzipped the flap and pulled the sides open. She emitted one little
squeak and clamped a hand over her mouth.

Mom, Frankie, and Sheriff Marge glanced at me, wide-eyed, then
scrambled to lean over Barbara.

Sheriff Marge scowled, jabbed a hand into the bag, and pulled out
a pack of bills. "How much?"

"I didn't count. I'd guess in the neighborhood of a million. Can
you hold the bags in your evidence room until Rupert decides what to
do with them?"

Mom balanced a leather pouch in her palm. "Is this—?"

I nodded. "Let's not open the pouches right now. They're starting
to disintegrate from age. But they hold gold dust."

Frankie looked as though she was struggling to breathe. "This beats
hosting fundraisers."

I chuckled. "I'm pretty sure this is a one-time-only deal."

Barbara plunked down hard on the floor, pulling the newspaper
clippings into her lap. She bent over them, delicately fingering the
crinkled edges. "I remember him, too," she murmured, pointing to the
picture of one of the mob lawyers.

I leaned forward. "Will you write down everything you remember?
Or I'll lend you a digital recorder if that's easier. I'm convinced Cosmo
was in some danger, maybe because of all this." I pointed to the duffel
bags. "He stopped by the vault the day before he died. I suspect he knew
his end was a real possibility and coming soon, otherwise he wouldn't
have produced the painting and donated it to the museum."

Barbara nodded slowly. "I'm not surprised. And, yes—yes, I will.
Everything I remember. I'll go through my father's things again, too.
Maybe now that I know—maybe something will stand out." She sniffed.
"I don't know if Cosmo was a good man or not, but he was good to me."

I squeezed her shoulder. "The vault manager remembers Cosmo, too, and he agrees with you."

OOO

Sheriff Marge phoned Dale for armed chauffeur service considering the value of what they'd be transporting. "Besides, I need a nap before dinner," she said. "Something Jesamie and I have in common. I want to fit in another picture-book session with her before they return to Chicago tomorrow."

"What are you reading?" I asked.

"Robin Hood." She peered at me over her glasses. "I know. We're already discussing the spirit of the law versus the letter of the law. My granddaughter will know the importance of both."

Dale pulled up to the curb and slung the duffel bags into the cruiser's backseat, behind the wire cage and auto-locking doors where they belonged. He returned to the sidewalk with an infectious grin on his face.

He lifted his Stratton hat, scratched, returned the hat, and grinned some more.

Sheriff Marge scowled. "What?"

Dale fished a few crumpled papers out of his pocket and handed them to her.

"What is this?" she grumbled, snapping them into orderliness. "What were you—" She pushed her glasses up and squinted to read through them.

"It's on the second page," Dale said. He waggled his eyebrows at me over the top of Sheriff Marge's head.

"You—you—" Sheriff Marge poked her finger at the paper. "This is the one?" She stared up at Dale.

He nodded, rocking on his heels, hands resting on his gun belt. "He claims he didn't know you wrecked behind him. Said he'd have turned around to help you if he'd known."

Sheriff Marge snorted.

"Judge Lumpkin's suggesting his fine be the price of a brand new SUV outfitted with everything you need," Dale added.

Sheriff Marge cleared her throat. "And you did this—on your own?"

Dale's Adam's apple bobbed, and he took a step back. "Well, Meredith gave me the tip."

Sheriff Marge whirled toward me, and my mouth dropped.

I shot Dale a thanks-a-lot glare. "I asked a friend—Maurice. You met him. Earlier. The Ferrari—remember?" I cringed under Sheriff Marge's stern gaze.

Sheriff Marge sniffed. "A new command vehicle, huh?"

"All the latest bells and whistles," Dale said, nodding.

Sheriff Marge frowned for a few more seconds, then thrust the papers back at Dale. "Good job. And you"—she jabbed a finger my direction—"tell Maurice I owe him a ride in the new SUV. He seems the type who'd enjoy that." She stumped around the car and sidled into the passenger seat, pulling her crutches in after her.

"Whew. She hates being out of the loop," Dale muttered out of the side of his mouth.

"She'll get over it." I grinned. "Just as soon as she gets that vehicle—with shock absorbers and springs in the seat and a back hatch that closes by itself without needing to be strapped down."

CHAPTER 22

Alex hustled Mom and me back to my trailer. He seemed worried we'd disintegrate if we didn't lie down pronto. I caught a glimpse of myself in the BMW's shiny exterior and realized my appearance might have had something to do with his concern.

I refused more Vicodin, though. I didn't want to be hazy for the family conversation, no matter how much I dreaded it.

I had no idea Alex was so handy in the kitchen, but he insisted on making us tea and toast and fussed about preparing ice packs and makeshift footstools and armrests. I could have gone for a big, juicy burger and fries, maybe a marshmallow milkshake, but I didn't think it was a good time to bring that up.

Mom slouched on the sofa and laid her head back, eyes closed. She massaged her shoulder through her bulky sweater.

"Hurt?" I asked, smoothing my skirt as far down over my purple monstrosity as I could.

"My arm aches from holding it against my body all day. I should have been moving it normally, stretching the muscles." She opened her eyes and smiled faintly. "I'm all right. Perhaps I needed this."

Alex hovered over her, a mug at the ready. Mom took the tea with her good hand and inhaled the steam for a few seconds before sipping.

Alex brought my tea next, then sank down beside Mom. She leaned forward, rested her mug on the side table, and took his hand. They sat still for a long time, Alex holding Mom's hand with both of his. I'd never seen so much overt affection from either of them. A good sign—awfully late, but a good sign.

Then I noticed tears sliding down Mom's cheeks, and my heart stopped. "Do you have cancer?" I blurted. "Terminal?"

Alex had a sudden coughing fit.

Mom straightened fast. "Cancer? N-no. Is that what you thought? Oh—" She let out a little laugh. "No, I guess it's not so bad, put in that perspective."

"Will you just tell me," I said through gritted teeth.

"Gambling. I have a gambling addiction. I've squandered"—Mom glanced at Alex and squeezed his hand until her knuckles were white—"almost everything."

"We'll manage," Alex murmured.

"How long?" I asked.

"After you went away to college. It started as something to do—a little thrill, a treat for myself to while away a few hours. It grew."

"I never knew."

"I made sure you didn't." Mom turned sad eyes to me. "I am very good at hiding things, as you well know. But the consequences have become too big to hide."

"We're taking measures," Alex said, returning to his normal business tone. "Austerity measures." He couldn't pull his eyes away from Mom's face. "It'll be like when we first married, and me fresh out of law school with loads of debt. Pork and beans for dinner, tuna casserole, date night meant a board game on the floor. Remember?"

"Are you ashamed of me, Meredith?" Mom could barely force the words out.

"Never," I whispered.

"Whenever you talk about this place—Platts Landing, the Columbia—you light up. I can hear it in your voice. It's a refuge for you, and I needed a refuge so badly, needed to be with you so badly for a while before facing"—Mom heaved a huge sigh—"the truth."

Alex wrapped an arm around Mom and let her cry on his shoulder.

Loud, obnoxious pounding made me flinch. Alex glanced up, but I waved him off—he had far more important things to do. I pushed myself out of the recliner and hobbled to the door.

Tiffany. In a pink foofy number that exposed just about everything on top, but with a skirt she could have hidden a string quartet under. It was hard to tell if she was playing Tinker Bell today, or a hooker. Or still covering an oozing rash.

"We're leaving," she announced.

"What a good idea."

"Not because we want to—well, we're almost finished with the documentary. But that cranky sheriff lectured us. And she strongly hinted we aren't welcome here." She sniffed.

"Ah." I wondered when Sheriff Marge had had time to fit that little bit of serve-and-protect into her schedule.

"Can you come down here?" Tiffany scowled. "I'm getting a crick in my neck."

If she hadn't noticed my leg by now, she wasn't going to. I did the sideways lurch-shuffle down the steps to my welcome mat, wincing. Now Tiffany could look down at me from the height of her stilettos.

"We had to wait until the state patrol finished asking questions, but they just told us we're free to go." Tiffany scraped at the mascara at the corner of her eye with a long fingernail. "So I guess I owe you an apology—or a thank-you."

I frowned. "What for?"

"For getting rid of our problem—Melvin's and mine. Melvin told me Vince was the one holding him to the grind. With him gone, we have a little more cushion to pay back the loan, and we don't have to find some crackpot piece of art."

There were so many things I wanted to say that I stood there with my mouth open while my thoughts shouldered one another out of the way at the tip of my tongue. Not the least of which was shock that Tiffany considered the death of a man the solution to her problem. I remembered Pete's assessment of her—the theatricality of her life. In Tiffany's world, all blood was ketchup. And that's when I truly felt sorry for her.

I finally came out with, "Why did you want the painting?"

Tiffany shrugged. "Melvin has this connected uncle who knew about some money stashed somewhere. He thought the key was in this crazy painting his buddy Cosmo Hagg made. Nuts, huh? But I remembered the painting from school tours—like I told you. We figured it was worth a shot. If it was a lot of money and nobody else knew about it, then we could pay off Melvin's debts."

"Uncle Juice."

"You know him? He's confined to a wheelchair now, but I guess he has quite a history."

"And he sent Vince?"

"No." Tiffany flicked her wrist impatiently. "Vince worked for the guys Melvin owes money to. I think he wanted to find the painting first, keep the money for himself."

"You know the painting's been destroyed, right? Completely ruined. It never was of any artistic value."

"The state patrol detective said something about water damage—or gouges? Anyway, I always thought it was a goose chase, the idea that horrible painting held the clue to a fortune."

So a few of the facts had been lost in Tiffany's translation, but I didn't feel the need to set her straight. "What's next for you?"

"Editing. Melvin will hole up in a studio in Burbank. He already has a line on the next film—an exposé of female Harley Davidson owners. Pete gave me the idea."

I sincerely doubted Pete had anything to do with Tiffany's inspiration, unless she'd happened to see his motorcycle. "Good luck."

OOO

Alex and Mom decided not to stay the night. Fair enough, considering the cramped dimensions of my sleeper sofa.

I gave them both the tightest hugs I could manage and extracted promises to call regularly. I even gave them a timeline—once a week, at the very least—both of them. I didn't care if they called together or separately, but I needed to hear Alex's more objective take on the matter and his assessment of Mom's mental and emotional state. She had a hard road ahead of her.

But my mother is one tough lady. And brave. She's pulled through worse than this before.

And, apparently, she knows a good man when she sees one. I was viewing Alex through a new lens, too.

I slept through everything that usually wakes me in the late summer—crows tussling with squirrels over the walnuts just starting to drop from the tree in the next campsite; excited children already zipping around the campground, the fat tires on their bikes whirring on the pavement; Tuppence clicking across the kitchen's hardwood floor to check if her food bowl has been magically filled during the night.

Her plaintive whine at the bedroom door was just filtering into my consciousness when there was a knock on the side of the trailer and a male voice shouted, "Flowers." A car door slammed and a vehicle drove off.

Flowers? That will get me out of bed any day.

I stumbled out of the bedroom, almost tripped over Tuppence, and opened the door to find a lovely bouquet balanced on the top step. The card said:

> Rest. That's an order. No more gallivanting about
> the countryside. I'm closing the Imogene for the
> remainder of the week, until we get things sorted.
> What would I ever do without you?
>   Rupert

Rupert's a great big teddy bear. I adore him.

Smiling, I dialed Frankie's number. "Did Rupert tell you the museum's closed?"

"Yes. He's called an emergency meeting with the entire board, Deuce Hollis—did you know the board has him on retainer as the nonprofit's counsel?—and a CPA Deuce recommended. He wants to resolve the legal issues surrounding Cosmo's legacy. They'll probably be locked away all day figuring out what the fine print says."

"Legacy," I murmured. What an excellent term for Cosmo's long-range planning. "I've been thinking about Barbara. Since we're not needed at the Imogene today, how about helping her clean up the salon?"

"Your truck's still at the museum, isn't it? I'll be over in half an hour to pick you up. I just need to put on my grubbies." Frankie hung up.

The idea of Frankie in any outfit less than perfectly pressed and accessorized set me to giggling. Tuppence's tail thumped against my leg—my good leg. She looked up at me with those melty brown eyes, whiskers twitching.

"Time for your morning constitutional?"

She snorted, and I let her out.

Coffee, oatmeal with toasted pecans and dried cranberries—life was returning to normal. It's amazing how great normal feels when life hasn't been normal for a while.

I sat on a kitchen chair and followed the hospital's checklist for cleaning my wound and redressing it. Much less purple. My leg was turning Technicolor with a little yellow and green. The entry and exit spots were starting to look like standard scabs instead of holes, with only traces of dried blood on the old bandage pads. Ticky-tacky. I chuckled to myself. Nothing like having Gemma tell you to suck it up—she's seen worse.

I rewrapped my leg with the pressure bandage and stood, testing my weight on it. Less hobbling today.

Then I called Mom and left her a good-morning message. No questions. Just an *I love you*.

ooo

The glass front door to Barbara's salon was propped open with a brass dachshund doorstop, and Hazel of the chili-recipe request stood on the stoop wringing out a mass of dingy cotton dreads in a bright-yellow mop bucket. She looked far too frail for such backbreaking work, but she whipped the mop around with her ropy arms, splashing water on my sandals.

"Barbara?" I asked.

"In the back." Hazel jerked her thumb over her shoulder. "Don't leave footprints."

Frankie tiptoed into the salon behind me.

Several of Barbara's regular customers bent with brooms and dustpans, sorting through the clutter on the floor, picking out the combs, clips, and scissors and sweeping up the rest.

Vince had been thorough. The sink at a hair-washing station had been smashed, and pieces of it hung precariously from the wall. I recognized the coveralled posterior of Jim Carter, local handyman, as he squatted in front of the pipes underneath, wrestling with a shutoff valve.

The mirror that ran the length of the room behind the styling chairs and counter had huge starburst cracks radiating out of spots where it had been hit with something hard and heavy. Barbara's till lay on its side on the floor, coins scattered everywhere.

"Barbara?" I called.

"Here." Barbara's bandanna-protected beehive popped around the corner of the back room. "Meredith, Frankie, I want you to have these." She loaded a stack of framed photographs into my cradled arms. "I think I'm through with them, considering." She fanned her face with a hand, her cheeks flushed. "And maybe they can work into a local history exhibit at the Imogene? I'll give you whatever related items I find in my father's effects, too."

"With all the money you helped recover for the Imogene, we could have an entire exhibit wing renovated," Frankie gushed.

I frowned at her over Barbara's head. Jumping the gun a bit there.

Frankie's lips pursed into a tight O. "Or maybe we'll have a few rooms painted," she backtracked. "Every little bit helps. You never know." She patted Barbara's arm.

"I'm just glad it's over," Barbara said. "Maybe now Cosmo can rest easy in his grave."

"What can we do to help?" I asked.

"You can finish taking these pictures down." Barbara pointed to the half-bare wall. "Dad didn't just hang them, he screwed them into the wall at each corner. Very thorough, that man. I'm thinking of moving the pedicure station to my other spare room, anyway." She grabbed Frankie's arm, parted the beaded curtain, and towed her out of the storeroom. "I want your opinion on a new nail polish display."

I grabbed a cardboard box that had been flattened and stashed next to the shop's back door and taped it up. But before I started loading it with Barbara's pictures, I checked the card in an enormous bouquet of red roses that sat on the little table between the pedicure chairs.

Platts Landing's propensity for busybodiness is rubbing off on me. I didn't plan on sharing the information; I was just curious.

Sure enough, the roses were from Rupert. But his note to Barbara was far more effusive than the note he'd sent me, and he signed off with an "XO" after his name. *Hugs and Kisses.* Mm-hmm.

Childhood friends seeing each other in a new light? The situation seemed promising. Maybe I could finesse a few things to encourage it.

I worked steadily, enjoying the activity after feeling so cooped up yesterday. Besides, wielding a screwdriver, sorting, and boxing are in my normal job description.

I hadn't noticed the ladies' chatter in the front room until it stopped. The hushed silence sounded as though they'd all been struck with sleeping sickness at the same time.

Then a few whispers, and one high-pitched, elderly voice piped up, far too loud. "She's in the back."

I was just stepping to the doorway to see what was going on when Pete appeared, a little flushed. Probably his first time ever inside a beauty salon. And certainly his first time figuring out how to deal with a beaded curtain.

I grinned. "You're back early."

"You weren't home—or at the Imogene."

"No." I shook my head slowly. "But I'm *here*."

"That's what I want to talk to you about."

There was a shuffling and chinkling behind Pete as the ladies jockeyed for better positions and became entangled in the curtain. We had an audience.

Pete's jaw tightened and he gripped my elbow, spun me around, and propelled me out into the alley through the back door, which he slammed behind him.

"Are we alone now?" he asked.

"For two seconds, if we're lucky."

He gathered me in, tight against his chest. I wrapped my arms around his neck and pulled his head down. He hadn't shaved in a few days and his cheeks were scratchy, but I didn't care.

He murmured against my neck. "When are you going to marry me?"

Footsteps pattered, and a muffled squeal came from the vicinity of the salon.

"How far is the Nevada border?" I whispered.

SHIFT BURN

An Imogene Museum Mystery
Book 6

After weeks under a Red Flag Warning and several flare-ups, the residents of Sockeye County, Washington, are on edge. When a fire threatens the Imogene Museum, curator Meredith Morehouse realizes the frequency and increasing size of the conflagrations aren't as random as lightning strikes.

Are the fires targeted? Are they vindictive revenge or a risky cover-up for something even worse?

Meredith already has her hands full with a brand-new endowment for shoring up the Imogene's crumbling foundation plus the imminent arrival of the most valuable collection Rupert Hagg, the museum director, has scored to date. And Meredith's hunky beau, Pete Sills, wants another kind of date—a nonnegotiable wedding date.

Can Meredith and Pete and cast-encumbered Sheriff Marge Stettler nail down the arsonist before their tinder-dry community goes up in flames?

1

Prickles crept inside my collar and along the backs of my legs. There's nothing like hallucinating that a convoy of army ants was on the march, and I was their parade ground. I gripped the steering wheel tighter to prevent futile scratching. This dry heat was getting old, and raising welts. It turned even the softest fabric against my crackling skin into torture.

I slammed my truck into park and hopped out, tugging my water bottle–laden tote bag across the bench seat after me. It was definitely a basement day, in spite of the construction crew's jackhammers. The Imogene Museum doesn't have air conditioning, but she does have thick walls, and her subterranean chamber was the coolest spot available. As the museum's curator, I have a never-ending checklist of unpacking, documenting, photographing, and organizing to do down there.

I was also in the process of spending a hefty chunk of the Imogene's recent endowment in the form of gold dust on foundation repairs for the old mansion. The parking lot was strewn with a mishmash of rusty and dented chipping, digging, smoothing, and mixing machines. Some of them looked like medieval torture devices with gears and spikes, claws, and tractor treads. They say any restoration project gets even messier before it gets better, and I wholeheartedly agree.

I had only an hour or so until the men who ran the machines would show up and turn the rest of the workday into something that sounded and felt like carpet bombing. The exhibits inside were covered with new layers of plaster dust every day as the building shook with the repair work. However, the old (built in 1902) girl was withstanding the inadvertent seismic testing remarkably well.

I sniffed. The past few weeks the air in Platts Landing has smelled faintly of smoke. A couple of large wildfires raged upriver. Hundreds of Department of Natural Resources and contracted firefighters had set up camp on the high school football field and at the county fairgrounds. They were working to exhaustion in twelve-hour shifts but not making much progress in containing the fires, which ripped through acres of steep canyons fueled by stiff winds and dead timber.

The past two nights, there'd been an orange glow to the northeast. Some said the fires were merging. No question they were moving closer.

I spun around, checking the barely green—thanks to the sprinkler system—grass in the county park. Something was wrong.

It took me a second to place the source of my unease—the silence. No birdcalls.

There's usually a busy chatter among the treetops when I arrive in the morning. Instead, I heard a quiet *phoooom*—a sucking sound, an inhale that didn't end. Then snap crackles, like a bowl of Rice Krispies.

I dropped my bag and ran.

NOTES

The Imogene Museum mystery series is a tribute to the Columbia River Gorge and the hearty people who live in gorge towns on both sides of the Oregon/Washington border. It's an extraordinary piece of God's real estate, and I savor driving, sightseeing, picnicking, and camping along its entire length. Hitching a ride on a tug run from Umatilla to Astoria is on my bucket list.

If you're familiar with the area, you may realize that I've taken liberties with distances in some cases. Mostly I squished locations (albeit fictional) closer together to move the story along and also to showcase the amazing geologic and topographic features of the gorge. In real life for many gorge residents, the round-trip to a Costco or a bona fide sit-down restaurant might well take a full day. This kind of travel time isn't helpful when you're chasing a fleeing murderer. But if you're not Sheriff Marge and have time to enjoy the scenery, the gorge is spectacular, and I encourage you to come experience it for yourself.

However, please don't expect to actually meet any of the characters in this book. All are purely fictional, and if you think they might represent anyone you know, you're mistaken. Really. I couldn't get away with that.

ACKNOWLEDGMENTS

Profound thanks to the following people who gave their time and expertise to assist in the writing of this book:

Debra Biaggi and BJ Thompson, beta readers extraordinaire.

Sergeant Fred Neiman Sr. and all the instructors of the Clark County Sheriff's Citizen's Academy. The highlights had to be firing the Thompson submachine gun and stepping into the medical examiner's walk-in cooler. Oh, and the K-9 demonstration and the officer survival/lethal force decision-making test. And the drug task-force presentation with identification color spectrum pictures and the—you get the idea.

I claim all errors, whether accidental or intentional, solely as my own.

ABOUT THE AUTHOR

Photo © 2012 Sarah Milhollin

I live in a small town in the west end of the Columbia River Gorge. When I grow up, I fully intend to be a feisty old lady. In the meantime, I regularly max out my library's lending limit, have happily declared a truce with the clover in the lawn, but am fanatical about sealing up cracks in my old house, armed with a caulking gun. Due to the number of gaps I have yet to locate, however, I have also perfected my big spider shriek.

I love wool socks, Pink Lady apples with crunchy peanut butter, scenery of breathtaking grandeur, and weather just cool enough to require a sweater, all of which are plentiful in the Pacific Northwest. I am eternally grateful to have escaped the corporate world with its relentless, mind-numbing meetings and now write (or doodle or fantasize or cogitate or stare out the window or whatever you want to call it) full-time.

I post updates on my website, www.jerushajones.com.

If you'd like to be notified about new book releases, please sign up for my e-mail newsletter. Your e-mail address will never be shared, and you can unsubscribe at any time.

I love hearing from readers at jerusha@jerushajones.com.